Paul Stuart Kemp
England in 1972. Na
his first published nc
in Great Britain by
second edition has become his third self-
published novel, and accompanies his other
work which is predominantly available over the
Internet. His official website can be found at
www.paulstuartkemp.com.

As an English writer, he has managed to resist
the mainstream American influence, and casts
dark tales throughout major British cities such
as London and Liverpool.

Paul Stuart Kemp lives in Berkshire, England.

also by Paul Stuart Kemp

Novels

The Unholy
Bloodgod
Ascension
Natura

Short Story Collections

The Business Of Fear

Praise for Natura - City of the Dead

NATURA

Paul Stuart Kemp

decapita

Published in Great Britain in 2001 by
Decapita Publishing
PO BOX 3802
Bracknell RG12 8FX

Email: mail@paulstuartkemp.com
Website: www.paulstuartkemp.com

Photograph of author by Helen Priest

The Author asserts the moral right to be
identified as the author of this work

First published in Great Britain in 1997 by Minerva Press

Second Edition: ISBN 0 9538215 3 6

Set in Meridien

Printed and bound in Great Britain by
Decapita Publishing
PO BOX 3802
Bracknell RG12 8FX

NATURA

CONTENTS

"The wise are not learned;
the learned are not wise."

Lao-tse
Tao Te Ching

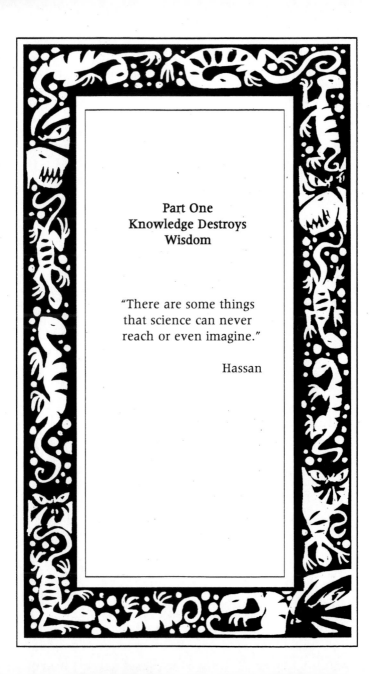

Part One
Knowledge Destroys
Wisdom

"There are some things
that science can never
reach or even imagine."

Hassan

ONE

WISDOM DESTROYS KNOWLEDGE

Overlooking the harbour of Hanoi k'Baja the Order of the Bening Tai'Orkha came together in secret. Their temple which had stood high in the Jume mountains for centuries had been razed to the ground only days before, bringing the Order into disorientation. It had been a deliberate fire, some said, started by one of the Order, a confederate of an antithetical religious group known only as Depurates. The Order was sworn to certain commandments primarily pertaining to creatures native to the Jume, who possessed bizarre abilities and it was claimed guarded and kept rule over Natura, the city of the dead. The Bening Tai'Orkha taught that these creatures took the human spirit once it had left its physical body into the city for judgement. The

Depurates contested this, mostly through violent and terrorist acts, protesting that these creatures be slaughtered to the point of extinction so that the human spirit be left free to roam the universe.

Only one thing was certain however. The destruction of the temple was the head of a war that had raged between the two sects for centuries. But there was also much controversy over the disappearance of the high priest; some said he had been seen praying inside the temple as the flames engulfed him; others said that he had fled with two of his disciples deeper into the heart of the Jume, taking with them the baby of a mad woman; others still told that he himself had gone mad and had travelled into the deserts of Nuba to find himself. Whichever of the stories was true was both irrelevant and unlikely ever to be resolved - the high priest was never seen again.

2

The street names were beginning to look the same now. With the ragged map she had been given in the same hand as her cigarette, Jessie tried her best to see through the rain-lashed windscreen. It seemed she had been driving around in circles for the best part of an hour, the address she wanted ever elusive.

There again on the left, Cromwell Road, she had been past that four times already, but according to her map that was where she needed to be. Indicating left, she turned in once more and slowed to a crawl along the narrow terraced street. The rain was coming down harder now making vision virtually impossible. Dropping the map on the seat beside her and putting her cigarette to her mouth, she reached forward and wiped the condensation to a smear and peered out into the night. And then as she pulled up at the side of the road, she realised why she had not seen Gallows Lane before. More an alley than a road and far too narrow for a car, its nameplate was blackened with grime and set low on the side of one of the houses. Pulling her collar up against the cold, she got out and set off into the unlit alley.

The thunder had ceased some time ago, but now it started up again and growled overhead. A strong wind picked up and whipped through the alley at her back, wrapping her wet hair about her face, blinding her with each gust. After maybe two hundred yards the alley suddenly ended at a brick wall, and she stood looking at it, confounded that it should even be there. Shivering as she wondered what to do next, she felt certain that the directions she had been given were correct, although the circumstances in which she had been given them were indeed cause for concern. North, he had simply called himself. She had stumbled across him near Ashen Bridge, lying on the embankment looking out over the river, and he had almost scared the life right out of her. It was a revelation even to her that she had spoken with him, telling him of what she was searching for. He had told her many things in return, and even now could not believe that she had taken his words like the teachings of a holy man. But now she was beginning to wonder whether she had just been victim to a vagrants insanity.

Turning round she started back the way she had come. She could see her old Volkswagon out in the road beneath the sheets of rain lit by the street lamps, the only comfort in a world of the unfamiliar. But before she had got maybe halfway back, she noticed a door set in the shadows of the dark brick wall, a door she was certain she had not seen before, and wondered if it was just the weather that had stopped her from seeing it.

Stepping towards it, she knocked twice, not altogether certain whether anyone would answer. The wind whipped at her hair again as she waited, and she pushed it from her face before knocking again. Leaning towards the door, she thought she could make out wheezing coming from the other side. She asked if anyone was there. The wheezing paused briefly, and then started up again.

"A man called North told me to come here," Jessie said to the door, listening intently.

She waited a moment, and then heard the rasp of bolts being drawn aside. The door opened a crack, and a craggy face appeared, its eyes squinting as it looked out into the gloom.

"I'm looking for somebody called Hassan," she told him.

The old man looked her up and down. She stood huddled against the rain, her arms wrapped around her, her hair plastered to her face.

"North, you said."

"Yes."

"And where did you meet this North?"

"In Hartwell," she told him. "By the river."

The old man seemed to muse on her words for a few moments, biting on his bottom lip, and then he said:

"You'd best come in."

Jessie followed him down a dark flight of steps into a room below lit only by a small fireplace that cast flickering shadows against the dull walls. She was glad of its warmth and eagerly took a seat by the fire when he offered it, spreading her fingers out towards the welcome heat.

"I am Hassan," the man confessed as she looked up. "What was it that North told you about me?"

"He told me many things about life," she started. "But he told me that you could tell me more."

"Life?" he said, as he settled into his own chair and began kneading tobacco into a small pipe. "You want to know about life?"

Jessie nodded, rain dripping from her hair.

He pointed his pipe at her. "Don't think about it, is my advice. Get on and live it."

She looked down at her lap, then into the fire, then back at the old man. He had lit a match and was sucking its flame into the bowl of his pipe. He glanced up at her.

"Why should you want... to listen... to what I have to say?" he asked her between mouthfuls of blue smoke.

"He told me you were a great man. That you could answer my questions."

"About life?" he asked her, puffing happily now.

She nodded. "Yes, about life."

"But why should you listen to what I have to say?" he said again.

"North told me that you were not a scientist."

"That's true."

"So how can you know about creation if you haven't studied or carried out experiments -"

"I never said I didn't study or experiment. Maybe not with bones and planets like scientists -"

"With what then?" Jessie demanded.

"With faith," he told her. "Have faith in the essence of life, it's all around you. You can't begin to understand life with a microscope or a tape measure. You have to feel it."

Jessie stared back into the fire, heaving a sigh.

"You're a scientist, aren't you?" he said, seeing her dejected in front of him. "I too know how it feels to lose everything you thought was right."

She glanced up at him, and said:

"I've always wanted to know what it's all about. Life, I mean. I thought science would show me the way."

"Science shows you nothing but facts. Relative facts."

"I know that now. For years I studied animal and plant genetics, trying to find out what it was that made life breathe. All I found was numbers. Life isn't about mathematics..."

Hassan leant towards her, his face serious.

"Then what is it about?"

"It's about..," she sought for the words. "Hell, I don't know what it's about, but it's not about mathematics." She watched as the old man bent to tap his pipe out on the hearth. "Ever since university, it was hammered into us that unless something could be proven with hard facts then it wasn't real."

"Sometimes facts aren't enough. There are some things that science can never reach or even imagine."

"That's why I suppose you need faith," she added. "To fill in the gaps."

"Even that is sometimes not enough."

Jessie got up from her seat and turned to leave.

"For the first time in my life I don't know where I should be going."

"I have no map to give you," Hassan told her.

"I know," she tried her best to smile but it was hopeless. "I see roads ahead but they are all unmarked."

"Fill them in as you go. You can do no more."

TWO

DIFFERENT WORLDS

Jessie closed the door of her apartment behind her and dropped her sodden coat to the floor. She wandered into the kitchen, shook the kettle, and then went to the sink to fill it. It was still cluttered with the last few days washing up, and she turned her back on it when the kettle was full. She stared out through the window as it boiled, at the solid darkness of the night, of the rain that was still heavy as it ran down the glass.

She felt too lethargic to think about what mood she should be in. She lit a cigarette and watched the blue smoke curl slowly up in front of her. Wandering into the living room, she slumped onto the sofa and curled her feet up under her. Her hair was still soaked and dripped as she ran her hand through it. It had been less than a week since she had walked out of the research facility, and she had gone from an up and coming young scientist to a lost soul wandering through alleys late at night. And for what? she wondered. She had thought she was learning about life, a real way of learning, a tangible way with facts and results. But in the end it was all a means towards getting a pay cheque and your picture in a journal. She wasn't even sure if that was why she had been so angry with Kelso for stealing that fame from her, or whether it was just because she really hadn't gotten any closer to the answers she was really after.

She remembered what Hassan had said to her: there are some things that science can never reach or even imagine. She had not understood this at the time but now it seemed all so clear. Had she really been wasting her time studying at the university, her years at the facility, when all she needed to do was just look at the world.

Stabbing the half-burned cigarette out in the already full ashtray on the coffee table beside her, she closed her eyes and lay back on the sofa as she blew the last lungful of smoke into the air. Her eyes were heavy and her mind ached from a week of fathomless questions. The kettle began to boil out in the kitchen, but she was already asleep.

The sound of traffic outside the living room window woke Jessie from her much needed sleep. She rubbed at her eyes with the back of her hand and glanced at her watch. It was nearly eleven in the morning. Getting up, she went into the kitchen to get something to put in her stomach. She made up her mind that she would go back to Ashen Bridge to find North again. It was probably luck - she wasn't sure if it was good or bad - that she had come across him on the embankment in the first place. To find Hassan's disciple once was one thing; to find him twice would be a miracle.

Seeing her coat in a wet heap by the front door, she took out a jacket from her closet as well as a scarf, before going out into the cold. The sun was bright outside, but the wind was bitter and damp from the previous nights rain. She was glad she didn't have to walk in such weather, and hurried to her old white VW parked a little way up the street.

The going was good, the traffic light at this

time of day, half an hour before the lunch hour started. Ashen Bridge was only fifteen minutes drive away and was one of the city's eight bridges that crossed the River Tye. This was the cheap side of the river. The side where the factory workers lived and the factory owners never strayed. The other side of the river had seen much in the last decade in the way of refurbishment and modernisation, where this side had slipped further into decline. Indeed Hartwell, the area around Ashen Bridge, was one of the poorest areas in the city. It was a home for the homeless, a community for the lost, a haven for the anguished. It was by no means an answer to their struggle, but at least it had a name.

The buildings seemed greyer as Jessie drove through the grimy streets of Hartwell. Litter circled along the gutters on the wind, a fog of fumes hanging in the air despite of it. One or two figures staggered along the pavements or stood in shop doorways like ghosts, their blank faces all but hidden from a world that had forgotten them. She drove past trying not to look at them in case it should seem she was judging them, yet she could not keep her eyes away. At each corner there seemed to be

27

another, discarded and lost.

She pulled up just before the bridge, and approached on foot until she came to the same gap in the railings that had led her down to the waters edge before. It was cold and damp and she dug her hands into the pockets of her jacket to keep them warm as she descended. It was also darker than she thought it would be as she made her way down a path trampled through the tall weeds of the bank, and felt a shudder of fear for the first time. She thought of the insanity of her being here, of her ending up a statistic on a police record when they at last dragged her battered body up from the bottom of the Tye. A week ago and she would never have even contemplated coming to such a place. But a lot had happened in the last week, and a lot of decisions had been made.

The embankment off to her left was deserted and as she reached the arch of the bridge, she stepped cautiously around until she could see beneath it. It was as dark as night here, and she could barely make out rough forms. She stood looking for what seemed like an age, but then she noticed movement beneath a heap of boxes.

Taking a breath, she gritted her teeth and took a step into the darkness. It was even chillier beneath the bridge as the wind blew itself into icy circles, cavorting detritus into weird spirals. The boxes continued to shuffle about as she approached. Jessie stooped forward as she walked. Lightly she spoke North's name.

The boxes stopped moving. It was almost black here beneath the bridge. She could not tell whether she could make out limbs behind the cardboard. Or eyes watching her. Reaching out a hand, she bent to lift one of the boxes. Her heart was thumping hard in her chest and in her head, the giddiness making her fingers tremble as she pulled one of the boxes to one side.

"North?" she said again. "Are you here, North?"

The cardboard parted and something came at her out of the darkness, a shriek at its throat. She dropped the box in her hand and stumbled back, loosing her balance and falling to the cold concrete. She clutched at her chest as her heart skipped in a frenzy, and saw the tail of a cat dart out and away up the bank.

Jessie sat on the concrete and waited for the tremors to go from her body until she tried to get to her feet. As she started back the way she had come, the boxes suddenly parted again and a shadowed figure stumbled from between them. Jessie cried out in alarm and stumbled back close to the waters edge. A guttural noise came from the figure that could have been either a growl or a cough, and by the way he couldn't manage to stay upright without staggering she could tell he was drunk, in fact probably near to comatose before she had stirred him.

"What are you wanting, woman?" His words were grizzled and spoken through phlegm. This was not North. This was what she hoped she would not find.

"Answer me. What do you want?"

"I'm looking for -"

"Speak up," he yelled, staggering towards her. "How d'you expect me to hear from over there."

"I'm looking for a man called North."

The figure stumbled closer. Jessie stayed where she was, paralysed with fear. As he moved into the partial light, she could make out his large rough features, most of which was covered by his huge matted beard, except for his eyes which seemed to be fighting hard to focus on her, the way they rolled in their sockets. She might even have felt pity for him if he wasn't scaring the hell out of her.

"North," he grunted. "And why would you be looking for him? You his daughter? Come to take him home?"

Jessie shook her head. "I just wanted to talk

to him?"

"Talk?" the drunk roared. "Fuck words. What good are they?"

"Do you know where I can find him?" she persisted. "He was here the other night."

"Well I'm here now," he said, a chequered grin of yellow teeth coming as he took another step towards her.

Jessie took a step in retreat but her foot found the edge, her heel dropping down towards the freezing waters swirling below. She looked to one side, to the bank she had come down, where the light from the cold day fell. He followed her gaze, and grunted a laugh before he reached for her.

She cried out as she toppled backwards away from him, but he managed to catch hold of her before she fell. He pulled her back, her balance still lost, and staggered back into the darkness amongst the boxes, stumbling to the ground bringing Jessie down with him. She tried to tell him to stop but no words would come from her throat, just sobs as he began pawing her and pulling at her clothes. Her arms reached up to push his bulk away, but he was heavy, and he was strong. The stench of rot and alcohol came upon her as she felt his coarse beard at her neck, his huge hands between her legs. She felt what strength she had go from her limbs, her chest stricken with panic and fear.

And then his rough hands went from her skin, his weight from her body. Her eyes opened through the haze of tears and she saw two figures silhouetted against the grey sky between the arches of the bridge. One was the cumbersome form of the drunk, the other a thinner figure, yet he seemed the stronger for he heaved the drunkard away and forced him to the ground. She sat up, pulling her jacket back around herself, and watched as the thinner figure began to kick the bulk slumped on the ground, each blow exhaling a moan.

Jessie edged away as the thinner figure left the drunk to his hurt and came towards her.

"It's okay," he said. "I'm not going to hurt you."

He held out his hand to her.

"It's okay," he said again.

She tentatively reached out and took his hand. He helped her to her feet and then led her out past the drunk, who was still lying clutching his stomach, and out into the daylight. He appeared to be somewhere in his early twenties and he said nothing to her until they were up the embankment and out by the roadside.

"What in God's name were you doing down there?" he asked her.

"I was looking for someone," she said, her arms still wrapped around herself to stop herself trembling, her eyes cast at the ground.

The young man lifted her chin up with his hand until she looked at him.

"You shouldn't be here," he said. "No matter who you are looking for."

"His name's North. I met him here the other night."

"I know a man called North."

"Can you take me to him?"

He nodded.

"My name's Luke," he said. "Come with me. I'll show you where he is."

Jessie left her car at the roadside and followed him across a small patch of waste ground and into a derelict building, its many windows boarded. It looked to have once been an office building, but as they stepped through a doorway she found it to be no more than a shell, its upper floor lying as rubble on the ground. There were several fires burning, their fumes thick on the cold air. And around some of these fires were the same faceless ghosts she had seen on the street, huddled in grey coats and blankets. From somewhere over near the far corner there came angry voices, shouting that everyone seemed to ignore, including Luke, who led her indifferently through the building. When they reached a doorway on the other side, she glanced back before stepping out into the open air again, and asked him:

"How long have you lived like this?"

"For as long as I can remember," he said airily.

Jessie could not think of anything to say to this. He looked across at her and smiled.

"We live different lives," he said. "How could I relate to any other world?"

They came upon a man lying face down amongst a line of bins. His coat was half pulled away, a pool of black blood beneath him. Jessie stumbled as she looked down at him, but Luke only broke his stride to see that she was alright.

"Is he..?"

"Dead?" Luke said. "Looks like it."

He took her hand and began to lead her away from the sight.

"Some people will kill for anything," he told her as they walked. "A knife in the gut for a cigarette, or a near empty bottle of whiskey. It doesn't matter to some people. Makes me sick."

"Does it happen a lot?" she asked cautiously.

"All the time," he said. "All the time."

Jessie said nothing. She glanced over her shoulder briefly to the body by the bins. How long, she wondered, before someone took his coat for their back, or his boots for their feet?

"Don't worry," Luke said. "You're safe with me."

She didn't feel convinced and her forehead remained knotted.

"Trust me," he said, smiling at her.

THREE

_____

WHAT CAME BACK FROM SPACE

L ines of fresh data filled the screen in front of Franklin Hoff. He surveyed it with much enthusiasm, like he had all the data that had come in since he joined the programme two months ago. He pressed a few buttons on the keyboard and the printer beside him whirred into life, filling a sheet with the text. Turning in his chair, he looked round for the head of the department.

"New data from the probe," he called across the room.

Robert Larson glanced up from one of the consoles. He scribbled a few notes onto his clipboard and then wandered over, tearing the sheet from the printer when it had finished.

"Good news?" Franklin asked, as he watched him look over it.

"Always good news from this probe," Larson replied. "It makes me nervous when things run to schedule."

Larson looked down at the boy studying him as he attached the sheet to his clipboard.

"Some of the probes we sent out in the early days tripped out and lost their co-ordinates; ended up roaming deep space like lost souls."

"But this one's okay."

"This one's okay," he said with a grin. "And it's just hit the Atlantic."

"When do we get it?" he was on the edge of his seat now.

"It's just a matter of hours."

Larson scrawled a few notes on the sheet. Franklin leaned a little to see better.

"It's an uncharted planet," Larson said suddenly, putting his pen away. "Nobody even knew it existed until a few years ago. We sent this probe out as soon as we had the budget. And now it's back."

All reports so far from the support crew had been that everything was intact, all sensors responding. He pressed his face to the glass eagerly as he saw the truck roll into sight, the container it was hauling long and grey.

"It's here," he said to himself. "At last."

By the time he had entered the decontamination bay the probe had already been winched from the back of the container and set in a chamber amid a host of mechanical arms. Technicians in radiation suits were already swarming around the re-entry scorched craft inside the sealed chamber, removing panels and dismantling the burnt shell. Another crew stood waiting with cables and computers, ready to strip the information from its carrier.

The Explorer research facility had been able to fund just one mission, and they had all known that if anything had gone wrong, or the probe tripped out like the last, then there could be no repeat. The probe had been meticulously constructed in order to get as much equipment inside it as possible, to record every conceivable detail. There had been video cameras to record the descent through the planets atmosphere as well as the landing, mining equipment to gather both soil and rock samples, sensors for air compounds and quality, measures for radiation, even a pulse satellite to leave on the surface to recommunicate with.

Larson went back up to his laboratory as the first data became available. He went into the video room once the discs had been sent up, and settled back to see the first close-up pictures of Calacenturae. His fingers were all but trembling as he punched the keys in front of him and the screens flickered to life.

Mesmerised he leant forward on the console as through the static he saw images of the virgin planet never before seen. The screen became choked with white as the probe passed through the dense atmosphere - Larson scrawled a note on his clipboard to check its composition from the readouts later - the anticipation seemed unbearable as the first glimpses of an unknown planet's surface grew imminent.

The probe burst through the final layers of misty cloud, the rocky terrain below thundering into view like a headrush. Stretched out below was a map of land and ocean, a mixed landscape of continents and river systems. The images inspired wonder at the birth of possibilities: could ingredients essential for life be found on a planet with an atmosphere able to sustain them? Larson picked up the handset beside him and called down to the decontamination bay as he watched the continued descent of the probe, its cameras now detailing imperfections across the land masses.

"When will the data cartridges be ready?" he wanted to know.

"Just taking them out now, sir."

"Can you have them sent up straight away?"

"I'll bring them up myself."

Larson replaced the handset and continued to study the screens in front of him. The probe was skimming the surface now. His heart sank as he saw the pictures relayed were those of desolation, bare rock and scorched earth. Leaning forward, he switched off the monitors and went back to the lab to wait for Franklin and the data cartridges.

2

What little there was on the desk in the top floor office had been arranged and rearranged during the numerous phone calls he had made and received all day. Anthony Kelso leant back in his large leather chair, pushing a few papers about in front of him, in the middle of another.

"It's just a simple case of you scratch my back..." he said, turning his chair round to look out of the huge panoramic window behind him. "We do each other little favours - that's how business works. I know I haven't been cashing the favours you owe me, I'm waiting until the time's right."

Kelso suddenly spun his chair back round and leant angrily on his desk, sending papers to the floor. His teeth began to grind as he listened, his temper starting to fray.

"Do you still remember who you're talking to?" he raged. "I've been supplying you for years so that your establishment can grow big on the money and the media." He picked up a pen and began to run it through his fingers. "Don't fuck with me, Emanuel. I have to take some of the limelight for myself or else I don't get funded, so don't act like it's the fucking end of the world."

Kelso slammed the pen back down on his desk.

"We need each other, Emanuel, you know that as well as I." A smile began to spread across his face as he listened, his perfect features glistening like oil once again. "The big one's just around the corner, I can feel it. And when it comes... yes, it's as simple as that."

"What do all these chemicals and compounds mean?" Franklin asked him, once the cartridges had been loaded.

"There are certain ones that are essential to life," Larson replied. "Like carbon and hydrogen. But there also needs to be others such as nitrogen, oxygen, phosphorus or sulphur."

"Could there be life on Calacenturae?"

"Not according to this readout," he said, pointing to the radiation count. "Any organic molecules would certainly have been killed."

"How would these molecules have got there?" Franklin asked, sitting up in his chair.

"There are countless theories," he told him, "but probably the same way as they got to Earth. They could travel through space, but would be killed by the solar winds that carried them. One of the theories, however, is that they could travel inside meteorites."

"And that could be how Calacenturae got all these elements," Franklin was grinning with excitement now, staring at the screen intently.

"If there had been the possibility of life, and cosmic radiation hadn't caused mass extinction of it," Larson continued, getting caught up himself now in the boy's runaway train of thought, "then who knows what we might have seen from the cameras? Might we have been facing a similar state to our own, with either human beings in control or an entirely new dominant species; and would we be able to cope with a world of the commonplace rather than the alien?"

The phone beside him rang and snatched them both from such fantastic supposition. He lifted the handset to be told that the mining pod had been removed and had been placed in a separate chamber. Larson replied that he would get to it as soon as he could and replacing the receiver, returned his attention to the monitor.

It was close to midnight when he at last switched off the computer and pushed himself away from the console. His legs ached with stiffness as he got to his feet, and he hobbled across the room to the window. He was the last one left in the building, the car park below deserted except for his own grey BMW. As he ran his hand through his receding hair, he remembered the mining pod. He cursed as he went back to the phone on the console. He dialled down to the decontamination bay but there was no answer. Not wanting to wait until morning, he switched off the lights to the lab and made his own way down to the chamber.

The decontamination bay was large, the lights flickering to life in rows along its length as he switched them on one by one. The knock of his feet echoed loudly off the walls around him like a toll as he stepped across the cold concrete floor towards the chamber the pod had been left in. Staring in through the large observation window, the pod sat like a large black egg, its exterior dull and uninteresting. Larson looked at it awhile, musing that such a thing should have touched the ground of another world, before approaching the controls of the mechanical arms.

The egg opened and Larson began to study the rock samples closely with the robot fingers, taking some aside for further examination. One of a number of larger slabs came up, sectioned and layered with different compounds. But it was as he was gently carrying one of them that it slipped from the grasp of the fingers. Unable to save it, it crashed to the ground, splitting apart in several places. Larson cursed as he studied the shards, their fragments less valuable now separated from each other. He went to return to the pod but one of the shards caught his attention for a moment. Leaning forward, he slowly guided the robot fingers towards it, gently picking up the shard and carrying it to the window in front of him.

Roughly the length of his arm, it looked like the carbonised limb of a tree. He wondered to himself if this were perhaps evidence of plant life on the dead planet after all, its shape nothing like that of the rock structure that had surrounded it. Placing it in a separate container, he unloaded it and held it in his hands for the first time. Returning to his laboratory, he began to test the composition of the limb.

His excitement doubled as his monitors fed him with information that confirmed his hopes; the limb was indeed organic. Studying the data as each new line appeared, his face began to drop. The limb had by no means once been part of a tree; the information in front of him proved that it had once had flesh around it, not bark - it had once been part of a body. The limb was not wood, it was bone.

FOUR

_____

MIDNIGHT REVELATION

Jerked from sleep as the phone rang, Jessie rubbed at her eyes and then rolled over, stretching out blindly to find it on the bedside table. She felt something slip from the edge and heard it thud on the floor. Her fingers eventually touched the familiar shape of the handset and she dragged it back towards her.

"Jessica?" came the voice on the other end. "This is Robert Larson. I've been -"

"Robert? It's the middle of the night," she said, pushing her hand through her hair.

"I know, but I've been trying to call you all week. Where have you been?"

"I've been out," she said.

"I haven't heard a word from you. You don't answer your phone. I've been worried."

"Thanks," she said. "But I'm alright. I've just

had things to do."

"I'm at the facility with the probe from Calacenturae," Larson said to her.

"It's back?" Jessie asked, sitting up in bed as she reached for the light switch.

"It certainly is," he told her. "I've been checking everything since it came back, and I've just found something unimaginable on board."

"Like what?"

"Like something I don't want to mention on the phone. Can you come down right away?"

"Robert, it's the middle of the night," she said again. She looked over at the clock on the table but it had gone, probably still on the floor where it had fallen. "What time is it?"

There was a pause, and then he said:

"Nearly two."

Jessie reached over and picked up the packet of cigarettes and her lighter from the table, lighting one and blowing a plume of smoke into the air.

"I'd really rather never set foot in that place again, you know that," she said.

"I know, Jessica," he said. "But I think this will be something you'll really want to see."

Jessie thought about it as she stared around

her cramped bedroom, her clothes still heaped on the floor where she had left them the previous night. The last thing she ever wanted to do was go back to that building, but she was feeling lethargic from her efforts with North and Hassan, and staying in her apartment now that she was awake seemed somehow depressing.

"Okay," she said at last. "Maybe I could do with some familiar scenery."

There was no traffic at all on the roads as she drove through Hartwell, the black streets lit only by the cold regularity of the street lights as she passed beneath them. She looked down at the clock on the dashboard - it was two twenty-five. The roads may have been empty but the sidewalks and shop doorways still had the same grey ghosts haunting them. She shivered as she looked at them, guilty that she was inside her car with the heater on full. She pitied those like the man by the bins, robbed of what little he had, including his life. But the boy she had met beneath the bridge had been right: worlds are so different from one another; how could either of them possibly relate to any other when they knew only of one.

The road took her towards Ashen Bridge, and she held her breath as she saw the iron railings where she had stopped the day before, and the unlit waste ground and embankment beyond them. Daylight had its share of dangers in the shadows, but the nightime had its own, and she prayed that her old car keep running to carry her away from them.

The Explorer research facility was on the outskirts of Morley, where the new industry was being built up, vast corporate headquarters of blue glass and glistening steel, a fine sight for those following in political spending, depending which side of the river you voted. It was a familiar journey that she had taken many times, but driving alone at two thirty in the morning she felt like a different species, searching for sustenance while everything else lay sleeping.

Every car park on the estate was empty except for one. She recognised Larson's old BMW and pulled up alongside, locking the door after her before hurrying across to the wide stone steps. She could see the security guard sitting behind the main desk in reception and tapped on the glass door until she got his attention. He looked up from whatever he was reading and eyed her with much suspicion. She saw him reach beneath the desk. The intercom beside the door clicked.

"Facility's closed," his voice crackled.

"I know it's closed. I've come to see Robert Larson."

"Facility's closed," he said again. "Come back in the morning. It's open at eight."

"I know it opens at eight, I used to work here. Can you just -"

The intercom clicked again and went silent. Jessie began to lose her temper and tapped once more on the glass door. The guard looked up again, glaring at her this time. The intercom clicked again.

"Can you call up to Robert Larson's lab," she said to him, "and ask him if he's expecting me."

She told him who she was, and he asked her to wait. The speaker clicked off again.

Jessie watched him through the glass door. It was getting close to three o'clock and it was freezing outside. She wrapped her arms around her as she watched him talk into a phone, wondering if any of this was worth it, and thinking that Larson would at least owe her a drink after all this. And to top it all, she thought, she had to beg to be allowed back into a building she'd sworn she would never return to. Life isn't about mathematics, she mused irritably, it's about coping with a string of tests designed to piss you off.

The intercom beside the door clicked again.

"Mister Larson says he's expecting you," the guard's voice crackled.

The door lock clicked open and Jessie stepped inside. He opened his mouth and began to tell her where Larson's lab was, but she told him through clenched teeth that she knew where it was, and strode past him without another word.

Even the corridors she had walked through maybe a thousand times or more suddenly seemed so strange, her footsteps eerie against the silence. Maybe it was because it was past midnight, or maybe because she no longer worked here, but either way she felt like she wasn't part of it any longer. The elevator took her up to the second floor, and as the doors slid open, she saw Larson waiting to greet her.

"It's good to see you again," he said, holding his arms out to her.

"It's only been a week," she replied,

hugging him warmly.

He told her that it didn't seem the same now she had gone, and that it felt like his daughter leaving home all over again. She smiled as they walked together towards his laboratory, asking him just what was so urgent.

"You sounded like you'd found the missing link or something," she said to him.

"Maybe I have, Jessica," he replied, stone faced. "Maybe I have."

She watched him punch in his security code at the entrance to his laboratory and then followed him in through the door. He led her across the room to a bench on which sat a small container with a glass front. He stood back to let her see for herself.

"What am I looking at?" she asked him, staring inside.

"What does it look like?"

Jessie looked harder.

"It looks like an old animal bone," she said. "A very dirty animal bone."

She looked up at Larson who was studying her intently. She began to shake her head.

"Where did you get this?" she asked him.

"From the probe, Jessica. It was mined from Calacenturae."

She stared back into the container, her head still shaking.

"Impossible," she stammered. "There's just no way -"

"I agree with you," Larson said to her. "But it's here; and it came from another planet. My planet."

Jessie looked round at him again.

"Why did you want me to see this?"

"I had to tell someone, Jess," it was his turn to shake his head now. "It hurt me when Kelso took the credit for your project. This could be your turn to take it back."

"This isn't some kind of tropical plant -"

"No shit," he said. "This is your chance -"

"My chance?"

"Yes. Your life could depend on this," he said to her. "This is big -"

"You're telling me it's big. This is huge. Monstrous. It's way too big for me. I'd never get away with it. Kelso would -"

"We won't tell Kelso."

Jessie turned away from him and began pacing about the room.

"How can we not tell Kelso?" she asked him, throwing her hands up in the air.

"Nobody else knows about it," he said.

"You can't keep something like this secret forever."

"Not forever, I know," he said, taking her by the arms. "But once your research is underway, he'll have to let you continue."

Jessie slumped down in one of the chairs and stared out of the windows at the night sky that was black except for the glimmering disc of the moon. How many times had she - or indeed anyone that had ever lived - wondered what it would be like if there was life out amongst the stars. Everything she had ever wanted was right here in front of her. But the biggest obstacle facing them, however, apart from undertaking such a massive task, was to continue without the head of Explorer learning of their deceit.

It was decided later that she should work alone at night using Larson's security card to gain access to whatever she needed. Nobody should be inside the building apart from the guard at reception, so at least that lessened the risk. Their only hope was that he wouldn't mention to anyone the creature who worked upstairs, searching for sustenance while everything else lay sleeping.

FIVE

SECRET'S OUT

A black Mercedes sped towards Morley in the balmy May night, its driver, along with his personal assistant, celebrating another appearance at Science Sphere magazines annual award ceremony. Pulling up at the rear of the building he let himself in at the back before heading straight to his top floor office.

"Another award, Mr Kelso," his assistant said, as she switched on the lights on her way to the leather couch.

"Indeed," he replied, tossing the trophy to one side before closing the door.

"What would you like me to do first?" she asked him, as she sat on the couch, pulling her black skirt up as she opened her legs a little. "Dictation? I could take something down for you."

Kelso dimmed the lights and took off his tie.

"Presentation first, I think, Emily," he said as he wandered slowly towards her.

The girl moved her knees farther apart as she hoisted her skirt up past her stocking tops to her hips, pushing the fingers of her left hand between her legs, exposing herself for him to see.

Kelso looked down at her, his face expressionless. Standing in front of her, he waited until she reached out her right hand, unbuckling his belt and pulling on his zipper. He exhaled deeply as she pulled out his erect member and began gently to stroke the sides with her fingertips.

"We shall have to see about giving you a raise," he stammered, as she leaned forward and ran her tongue over it.

She glanced up at him, smiled, and then slid her mouth down over him.

Kelso grabbed hold of the back of her head as he watched her rhythm at his lap. His eyes began to flutter shut, his breaths now heavy in his throat, when a light through his office window distracted him momentarily and he looked up. The growing sensation in his groin had virtually taken him over completely, but he forced himself a second look out the window. A car had pulled up outside, the glare from its headlights filling the room.

Kelso knew it was close to midnight. Nobody was supposed to be in the building, not even he. He had lost the urge in his balls and he pulled away from Emily's lips. She spluttered on her drool as he withdrew and looked up at him.

"What's wrong?" she asked, wiping her mouth with the back of her hand.

Kelso ignored her and walked over to the window, zipping himself back up as he looked down into the car park. A white Volkswagon had pulled up below, and he watched as somebody got out and hurried towards the building and out of sight. He couldn't make out who it was in the ill-lit car park and turned and picked up the phone on his desk.

Emily had seen the headlights roll across the ceiling, but now she saw Kelso's anxiety, she got to her feet and smoothed down her skirt.

"Who is it?" she asked, as she went to him at his desk. "Your wife?"

Kelso ignored her and punched a few numbers on the phone.

"Security? Who was it that just came in?"

Emily stood beside him and watched as his face scowled.

"Who is it?" she asked again.

This time he answered her.

"An old worker," he growled.

Slamming down the handset he stormed from the room.

Emily watched him go.

The guard in reception looked up from his book as he came through the door, all expression dropping from his face. Kelso stepped up to him, his eyes narrowed, and leant across the desk in an almost casual manner.

"What's your name?" he asked the guard.

"Brooks," the man stammered. "Cordell Brooks."

"Well, Mr Brooks," Kelso said, leaning even further towards him. "Can you tell me how somebody who no longer works here, can come to be in the building?"

"You mean Miss McHard?"

"Of course I mean Miss McHard," he yelled.

Brooks was trembling now, but remembering his six weeks of training he tried to continue in a steady voice. "She has a security pass," he said. "I assumed -"

"Assumed what? That you'd still have a job when I eventually found out?"

"No," his book dropped from his fingers and tumbled to the floor. "I assumed she'd been taken back on."

"Well, you were wrong on both points," he told him. "Pick up your shit and get out of here."

"But Mr Kelso," he protested, his eyes wide, "they told me they were working on a secret project."

"They?" his voice softened.

"Yes. Her and the other scientist."

"What other scientist?"

"Larson," he said. "Robert Larson."

Kelso closed his eyes and turned away from the desk. Breathing a sigh, he asked:

"You didn't think to mention this to anyone?"

Brooks shook his head. "They said it was okay."

Kelso turned back and pursed his lips.

"What else haven't you told anyone?"

Brooks looked down at one of his monitors, and fiddled nervously with one of his pens.

"How long has this been going on?" Kelso demanded to know.

He glanced up. "About eight weeks," he said quietly.

"Eight weeks?" he raged. "What the fuck am I paying you for?"

Turning on his heel he hurried from reception.

"Am I still fired?" the guard asked, as he got to his feet.

"Count yourself lucky you're still breathing," Kelso retorted over his shoulder.

With a single lamp to work by, Jessie sat in front of a computer and punched keys furiously, glancing across frequently at a number of different instruments scattered around her. She muttered to herself as new lines of data appeared on the screen, until she could barely suppress a whoop of joy as the screen literally rolled with pages of information. Sitting back in her chair, she took up her cigarettes and watched her months of effort appear from behind a haze of blue smoke.

As the information rolled to completion, she slipped a disc into the drive and saved the final stages of her work. Looking back, she knew it had been nothing but luck when she had dropped the bone from Calacenturae, although at the time she had almost died of fright certain that she had broken it. A reddish brown substance had appeared at the crack and testing it, had found it to be intact marrow. This discovery she had made on her own. This had been her work. She had been running endless tests until now she had the bones DNA structure; and it was listed in code almost entirely in front of her. There had been times of sheer guesswork when she had looked at strings of genetic code that made no sense to her - in fact there were still strains of it that made no sense to her - but she would have to study these further.

From outside the lab, she heard the elevator open in the silence of the empty building. Stabbing her cigarette out on the table, she leant forward and turned off the screen in front of her before flipping the switch on the lamp, sending the whole room into darkness. Jessie sat where she was, her eyes straining towards the door, but they were still swimming with the echoes of the glare of the screen and she could make out nothing.

She heard the click of the lock as a security pass opened it. It wasn't one of the guards, she thought; there was no searching beam of a flashlight. The colours in front of her eyes were beginning to subside and she could just distinguish a figure moving slowly across the floor. She became aware for the first time that the moon was casting its pale light in through the windows, and if she could make out the shapes in the lab, then so could he.

Realising that she was sitting near the middle of the room, Jessie thought about getting out of her chair to hide somewhere more discreet, or even perhaps making a run for the door. But any movement now, she guessed, would mean certain capture. She followed the figure round the room, and in the moonlight could see him looking intently around the benches. He was looking for her, she was certain of that, but why did he not have a flashlight? But then he called out to her.

"I know you're in here," he said.

Oh God in Heaven, she said to herself. It was Kelso.

"I know you're in here, Jess," he said again. "You may as well come out."

Great, she thought. It was Kelso and he knew she was here. It occurred briefly to her that he could just be guessing, but he wasn't the guessing kind. He knew.

She reached over and flicked on the light, and watched as he turned towards her. She wasn't sure what his reaction would be. Rage certainly, or even threats. But the one she got was the last she would have expected. He started towards her with a smile on his face, and it grew bigger as he approached. She hadn't been certain what her own reaction would have been when she saw him again, perhaps the same as she had expected from him, but it surprised even her when she remained calm, even when he sat beside her on her desk.

"Long time, no see," he simply said.

She looked up at him, confounded as to what to say.

"So what have you been up to since you left?" he asked her. "Besides coming here for the last two months."

Jessie bit her lip. He had her dead to rights and they both knew it.

"Well?" he said, picking up her cigarettes and looking at them. "You must be studying something. You always were unstoppable when you were on to something big."

"Shall I tell you so you can take all the credit?" she said bitterly.

"You're not still on about that, are you?"

"It was my work you stole."

"I sent you to South America," he said, indignantly. "I supplied everything."

"But you didn't do the work that counted."

He smiled at her. The bastard smiled at her.

"I've got your award upstairs in my office if you want it," he told her.

"Eat shit," she said, snatching her cigarettes back.

Kelso got up from her desk and wandered about, looking at all the instruments laid out around her. The bone was sitting in the glass-fronted container on a bench further away, and her heart sank as she watched him walk towards it. He stopped and looked inside. Jessie could feel her research slipping away just like the last, Kelso's hands slowly reaching around it like a greedy child ready to snatch it away again. Then he turned round to look at her.

"It's this, isn't it?" he said.

Jessie said nothing. Everything was about to be taken away from her, and her words would only quicken the departure.

"Tell me what it is," he demanded.

Jessie kept her silence.

Kelso started back towards her. "This is the

only chance you'll get to keep whatever it is you're doing here. Now tell me what it is."

"Why should I tell you?" she said.

"Because I can have you shot as a intruder for illegal entry. Or I can kill you with my own hands now. So tell me what it is."

"I want to be allowed to carry on with what I've started," she reasoned.

"I'm not saying you can't. I just want to know what it is that's so secret."

Jessie took a breath and stared past him to the bone in the container, to the source of what was to be her future.

"Unless you'd prefer that I talk to Robert Larson," Kelso added.

She looked back at him.

"No," she said quickly. "Please, leave him out of this." She glanced back at the container briefly, then back at Kelso. "It's a bone. Larson's probe brought it back from Calacenturae."

Kelso's eyes widened.

"All that probe brought back was dust and radiation," he said.

"No," she told him, shaking her head. "It brought that back as well."

Kelso began to pace up and down in front of her, his jaw locked solid, his face full of anger.

His eyes seemed to flicker as if a million decisions were being made behind them. Jessie contemplated making a dash for the door again, but she knew she could never make it. Then he suddenly stopped and looked back at her.

"How far have you got?"

She hesitated, glad that she had turned off the screen so that he couldn't see for himself.

"Tell me, woman, or I swear that I'll -"

"Superficial study," she said.

His eyes narrowed, but the gaze was still fierce.

"I could get technical..." she continued.

He silenced her and went back to have another look at the bone.

"You've done nothing of any merit so far?" he asked her, turning to see her shake her head. He took a breath. "Write me a report of what you've done so far and let me have it by the end of the week."

"Then you'll make a decision about letting me continue my research? I think you owe me that much at least."

"Yes," he nodded. "And I know somebody else who still owes me too."

LEGEND'S BORN

Jessie left the television and went into the kitchen. The news was pretty mundane these days, she thought, as she pulled bread from the refrigerator. The same stories of wars and murders, abroad and at home; the bite softened after a while. Opening one of the cupboards, she pulled out a tin of beans, and turning to see the saucepans still dirty in the sink, put it back where she'd found it. As she buttered the bread, folded it in two and began to eat, a knock came at her door.

"I got your message. I came as soon as I could," Larson said, shaking the rain from his coat before stepping into her apartment. "What's going on?"

"Kelso is what's going on. He caught me last night."

"And?"

"I'm still breathing aren't I?"

Larson followed her through into the kitchen and watched her butter a second and third slice, offering him a share of her breakfast.

"Want some?" she asked him.

He shook his head.

"So what about Kelso?" he continued. "What did he do?"

"Surprisingly little. He got real mad when I told him about the bone."

"You told him about the bone?"

"I had to. I wasn't sure what he'd do, and he'd believe nothing but the truth."

Larson leant against the counter and rubbed his face with his hands.

"I think it might be alright," she told him. "He seemed okay when I left him."

"Okay? If there's one thing I know about Anthony Kelso it's that he's never okay."

"He asked me for a report on what I'd done. Said he'd decide whether to let me continue or not."

"And you believed him?" His expression was incredulous.

"I had no choice," she said, as she put the bread back in the refrigerator. "If I hadn't done what he wanted I could be in jail for trespass, or buried in a hole somewhere."

"I guess you're right. I should never have started this -"

"We did this together, remember?" she said.

"Then we'll take the consequences together."

They tried their best to comfort each other with a smile, but in the silence they heard the drone of the television from the other room. More precisely, it was the news story that caught their attention.

Jessie dashed from the kitchen, Larson a step behind her.

...where fire-fighters have the blaze relatively under control. As yet no casualties have been confirmed, the explosion coming after the building had been evacuated by police who received a bomb warning earlier today from activists...

Jessie dropped onto the couch, agog as she stared at the small screen.

...laboratories at the Explorer research facility completely destroyed, a spokesman condemning the act as sheer vandalism by natural rights groups...

"No," she sobbed. "How could this happen? Not now. I was so close."

Larson sat down beside her and laid his hand on her shoulder.

"The bone's destroyed," she said through a veil of tears. "It would have been better protected if I had done this properly. I took responsibility for it. And now it's gone."

"The whole building was a target," Larson told her. "There's nothing you could -"

"Don't tell me that," she said. "I don't want to hear it."

She pushed herself to her feet and watched the flames pour from the windows of the laboratory behind the reporter.

"So it's all over then," Larson said to her, switching off the set.

"Everything at the lab, yes," she replied. "All I've got left is the disc."

"What disc?"

"I completed the final bit of DNA code last night. I saved it to disc just before Kelso arrived."

"Where is it?"

"Over there," she said, pointing to her jacket. "But there's something about it..."

"What, the disc?"

"No. The bone's genetic structure," she told him. "There's parts of it I've never seen before."

"What do you expect?" Larson said. "It's from another planet."

"No, it's more than that. There's something strange about it."

Larson got to his feet and made for the door.

"I'm going down there," he told her. "To see for myself. Want to take a look?"

"There's nothing to see," she said. "Not any more."

Jessie closed the door behind him and then went over and took the disc from her jacket pocket, before sitting down in front of her computer. She plugged the disc into the drive and waited for it to load.

Looking out of the window beside her she could see that it was beginning to brighten up, the rain clouds overhead parting after the mornings deluge. It was quiet out in the street below, only the occasional car passing. But then she saw somebody lurking on the pavement a little further up. In fact she would not have even noticed him except that he was leaning against the railings, his hands stuffed inside his jacket pockets, staring blankly up at the sky. As she leaned closer to the window he looked up at her, but she recognised him before he could turn away. Getting to her feet she dashed across the room and out of her apartment, leaping down the stairs and out of the building. But by the time she was out in the street Luke was nowhere to be seen. She stared up and down but she couldn't see him, although she couldn't be certain whether he had fled or simply found a better hiding place. Whichever it was she couldn't help wondering, as she returned to her apartment, why he should be watching her at all.

Closing the door behind her, she glanced back out at the empty street before returning to her computer. There were other mysteries that needed to be solved; a boy outside her window was just another that would have to wait.

"Okay," she said out loud. "Let's see what secrets you've got."

2

Hobart Weiss whistled as he marched through the Axis News building and on into the crew's control room. Max was winding through a mountain of video tapes as Angel directed his efforts over his shoulder. Slouched at the back, his feet up on the table, sat the crew's driver

Daytona, a crumpled comic book in his hands.

"Where have you been all morning?" Angel asked him, glancing up.

"Only trying to secure the biggest news story of the year," he countered with a flourish.

Angel turned to face him and stuck her hands on her hips.

"And what might that be?"

Hobart stepped about the small control room, attempting to build his moment of glory. Even Max had turned to look at him now. Daytona still had his head buried in his cartoons.

"Out with it," said Angel impatiently.

"I take it you're familiar with Genepool," he started.

Angel nodded. "The bio-engineering company. What about them?"

"Well, what if I were to tell you that they've been working on an old bone to the point of cloning."

"They've been doing that for years, Hobart. I don't see -"

"And what if I were to also tell you that the eggs they've engineered are close to hatching."

Angel shook her head.

"It's interesting," she said, "but we need

news here, remember? Hard hitting -"

"How hard hitting would aliens be?"

Max looked from Hobart to Angel, then back to Hobart. He knew what kind of temper lay behind her endearing face, and he also knew it wasn't good to be around when it broke. He began to get anxious as the inevitable came - her hands behind her back, she started to pace the control room.

"You're our top reporter, Hobart, you know that. And you also know that we are not some cheap shit rag people pick up at check-outs. We're a professional news crew, get it? Top line. If you can't cut it any more -"

"Listen to me, Angel," Hobart insisted. "I've been with Victor Emanuel, head of Genepool, all morning. He's promised us exclusive rights with these eggs. They're from another world. I don't know all the details, but they came back in a space probe or something. These are real aliens."

Angel stopped pacing and looked hard at him. Her expression was as intense as his. Even Daytona had stopped reading to peer over the top of the pages of his comic book. Max hadn't moved throughout, but now he shifted in his seat as her face softened a little.

"If you're shitting me..."

"I'm not," he said, grinning. "I promise. This story will make Axis News the biggest in television history."

"And if it doesn't, I'll string you up by your balls until you wish you'd been born a eunuch. Daytona, get your keys."

"You're sure this area is secure enough?"

"Look, Highwater, there are only two doors in. One here, and one at the other end of the compound, and that only leads to the boiler room."

"But what if -"

"They've both got fail-safes," Kinard reassured him. "Ain't nothing gonna get through there, believe me."

Highwater looked down at the steel door and the mechanism attached to it.

"I just don't know," he said, shaking his head. "There could be anything in those eggs. These are aliens after all."

"E.L.F.s"

Highwater looked up at him.

"Engineered Life-Forms," Kinard explained, smiling.

"Well, whatever the hell they are, it's my job to make sure they stay where they're supposed to stay. If security in this place is breached -"

"Trust me," Kinard told him, staring down into the compound below. "Your job is quite safe."

The door behind them opened, and a flamboyant man in a dark suit strode towards them. Kinard shook his hand.

"Good morning, Mr Emanuel," he said to him. "Everything's running to schedule."

"Excellent," the man replied, glancing out through the window at all the activity in the chamber below. "When do you expect the hatching to begin?"

"Any day now. The technicians have reported movement inside and -"

"There'll be a news crew arriving at some point," he said, straightening his tie in his reflection in the window. "I trust we can accommodate them somewhere close to the action to record the entire event."

"You didn't mention..." Kinard started. Emanuel looked round at him. "I guess I can find some room for them down on the floor," Emanuel smiled and checked his reflection again, "but space is limited."

"I can't begin to tell you how much this all means to the company," he told him. "Recording history; and us along with it. Money. Fame. Immortality. We're stepping into the unknown."

"Do you know what lies inside those eggs?" Highwater tested.

"Of course I know what lies inside," he told him, grinning. "Legends."

SEVEN

AND ONCE AGAIN

The lines of data kept coming. No matter which way she tried the calculations the same codes appeared in front of her, and the realisation that what she had found had been correct all along was setting like concrete. Jessie slumped back in her chair and stared at the screen in her apartment, fearful of what it was she was actually looking at. It's true that when she had extracted the DNA from the bone, there had been other lines of code she had not recognised, could never recognise, the source of which being completely foreign not just to her but surely to anyone on Earth. The bone may have been destroyed along with the rest of the laboratory equipment, but she still had the disc and she had continued to research those mysterious codes from it.

It had been sheer curiosity that had driven her to study and check, study and recheck those codes, but now she had deciphered so much more of the data she had become afraid. There were things hidden here, she knew, that no one on Earth could possibly comprehend. Her thoughts drifted to Hassan and to North with their doctrines, and how they thought they were aware of so much. Flesh and fire, sky and earth; these were the things of which they spoke. But hidden within the bone were secrets, she was more than certain of that, secrets beyond the scrutiny of any microscope or tape measure, and she was sure that she now had more within her reach than even they could imagine. And if these secrets were to be found in such a fossil, then what of the creatures from which it came?

Jessie read and re-read the lines of code like she had done for the last few days. There was mystery here, she knew; mystery and power, the proportions of which she thought she might never comprehend. With the bone destroyed she could prove nothing. All she had was the initial data she had drawn at the time; there could be no re-test or re-examination. And yet this was all real. The bone had been part of something alive. There was other life in space - or had been some other life in space - there was proof of that now, something with energies far greater than those of man.

Switching off her computer she hurried from her apartment and went out to her car parked in the street. It was late in the afternoon and she needed to tell someone else before she lost her mind to the labyrinth of supposition.

Leaning back in his leather chair, Anthony Kelso looked out through the large window and watched the trucks come and go outside. The reconstruction of the west wing was nearly complete, but he spared hardly a thought towards it. All he could do was wait for the phonecall. There was hardly any sign of bomb damage left, apart from in the memories of a few, and even they would pass in time.

Sitting and waiting, he mused over his last two decades. He had built his company on the back of a single scientist, Clay Munroe, whose amazing discoveries he had turned into lucrative ones. Munroe was gone now, but it didn't matter; his discoveries had been made for the Explorer research facility, and he now had several top scientists to take his place, scientists who had unwittingly been searching for the ultimate discovery.

Of course there was much to be made from knowledge, he had always known that. And he had soon learnt that it was who you could sell it to that was the most exciting part - and in this business, it was the media mostly. Of course at first it had been the journals he had sold to, but once he had discovered contacts in television, the sky had been the limit.

The intercom buzzed on the desk behind him, snatching him from his memories.

"Yes, Emily, what is it?"

"There's a call for you. Mr Emanuel from Genepool. Do you want to take it?"

"Yes, of course I'll take it," he said eagerly. "What line?"

Larson was waiting for her by the lift. He was thankful there was no one about and that she was alone in the elevator when she got out.

"Jessica, what are you doing here?" he said to her urgently.   "Kelso'll have your head if he sees you."

"I had to speak to you."

"The bone?"

"What else," she replied. "Is there somewhere we can talk privately?"

"I don't think that would be in anyone's best interests, do you?" Kelso said, smiling into the handset. "No...we can't be seen to be blowing up our own companies." He began to laugh at the other man's humour. "Take your glory, Emanuel, and the money as well. It'll be no good to me."

Kelso leaned back in his chair and swung his feet onto the desk.

"But this *is* business," he said, "and no thanks are necessary. I'll watch for you on prime time."

No sooner had he replaced the receiver than the intercom buzzed again.

"Yes, Emily, what is it now?"

"MacKensie in reception called up a few minutes ago, he said you wanted to know if Miss McHard came back."

"She's here?"

"Yes, sir. Apparently came to visit -"

"Robert Larson," he finished.

"Yes, Mr Kelso."

He clicked off the intercom and went to the window. Parked outside was an old white Volkswagon.

Larson sat wringing his hands, shaking his head at what Jessie was asking of him.

"There's just no way," he said to her. "You want the impossible."

"But can't you see it's the only way?" she implored.

"I know it's the only way," he said. "But another probe? How do I sneak another probe past Kelso."

Jessie got to her feet and started to walk in circles around the table. She knew she was asking for miracles, and standing here and now, wasn't even sure why she had even come to him. Maybe it was because he was the only one who was on her side, or maybe because he was the one who had started the whole nightmare. But looking at him now, close to breakdown himself, she knew he could do nothing for her.

"I think your only hope lies in your antagonist," he said to her under his breath.

She turned to look at him.

"Kelso?" she said.

"Only he can do what you ask."

"I think you're forgetting -"

"I'm forgetting nothing," he said. "But what can I do? If you want to research further, you'll have to go to him."

Jessie breathed out her hopelessness and went to look out of the window. They both turned their heads as the door opened behind them. Larson started to his feet but Kelso was beside him pushing him back into his chair before he was halfway vertical.

"Just what the fuck is going on around here," he hissed at them both.

Jessie and Larson exchanged glances across the room.

"Answer me," Kelso raged. "And give me the fucking truth. You, McHard," he said, pointing at her, "Why are you back?"

"I had to speak to Robert," she said.

"You've never heard of phones? What did you have to speak to him about?"

"The bone," she said, glancing furtively at Larson.

"What about it? We don't have it anymore."

"I carried on researching the DNA I had extracted -"

Kelso winced.

"- I had all the data on disc. There's something not right, Anthony, not right at all. And if I could study it properly I'm sure -"

"You need not worry about all that any more, Jessica," Kelso said to her. "You see, other scientists have also carried on with their work, and the fruits of their labours will be unveiled very soon."

"What are you talking about?"

Larson got to his feet; truths were dawning here.

"Genepool have cloned a batch of eggs from the bone's DNA, and they're just about ready to hatch."

Jessie was trembling now, stumbling towards him.

"How did they get the bone?" she demanded to know.

Kelso smiled at her.

"The activists must have stolen it," he said, "before they destroyed all your equipment."

Her eyes were stinging with sudden rage and rolling towards him, took a swing at him. He dodged her blow with surprising ease and took refuge on the other side of the table.

"You're a good scientist, Jess," Kelso said to

her. "But don't even begin to think that this is in your league. That bone was what this company was built on the back of. That bone is my whole life. Your strength is admirable, Jess, but I just couldn't take the risk."

She started after him again but Larson held her back.

"If you want to see history in the making," he said, "then I suggest you watch the news."

"You don't understand," she said to him, her teeth grinding. "There's something wrong in the DNA patterns. No one can be sure what these creatures are."

"Don't be so quick to hold onto what you think you know; naivety might be your undoing. Besides, I'm sure the scientists at Genepool know -"

"What do they know?" she shouted at him, throwing herself across the table at him. "What can they know about an alien species? Something powerful's in those eggs; and you'd better hope to God that they're friendly."

EIGHT

_____

DEVILS, NOT ANGELS

There was precious little room for the equipment they had brought with them, but they set up what they had between the pumps, monitors and incubating equipment camped around the nest of eggs, most sitting dormant but for an occasional flicker or beep. Just over a foot in length, each egg was a mottled dull grey. The half dozen that Genepool had engineered were sitting inside a sealed reinforced glass container, a number of cables and hoses attached around its base.

Left to his own devices while the rest of the crew recorded background material around the building, Daytona finished double-checking the hardware. There were possibly four or five technicians in long white coats wandering about the compound going from console to console. They paid him little, if any, attention at all, for which he was glad for it left him free to scrutinise what lay waiting inside the glass container.

He'd overheard bits of so many conversations all afternoon that he felt like even he was perhaps some kind of an expert on the subject. He had seen the magazines in check-outs the same as everyone else that told of housewives alien encounters and men from Mars - had bought some of them too - but standing there looking at real alien eggs made him want to heave; this was science fiction gone ape-shit. The secrecy and security he had seen already was way too much for this to be just another hoax of magazine proportions, and he couldn't decide whether the luck that had brought him here to witness it all was good or bad.

He leant forward and pressed his face against the glass, the large eggs like props from a cheap science fiction movie. As he tapped the container with his fingers, one of the machines wired to it whirred into life and began to beep. Leaping back he flung his hands in the air in innocence. Two of the technicians looked up from their monitors at him, the others kept their heads buried in theirs. Something caught his attention and he glanced back down into the container. One of the eggs was moving.

A technician was beside him before he could say anything, pushing past to boot machines and punch buttons on control pads. Daytona couldn't take his eyes off the eggs as they each in turn started to rock and tumble. Stumbling back, he reached into his jacket laid across a tripod behind him, pulled out his phone, and punched in a number. Hypnotised by the scene before him, he stared helplessly as it connected.

"Angel," he said, his eyes still hard on the glass container. "Angel, it's me. You'd better get your asses down here... never mind any of that," he pushed his hand through his hair. "Hell's a comin', Angel... No, I ain't shitting you. Get down here now!"

He dropped the phone at his feet and fumbled to set the camera up on the tripod in front of the container. Max had shown him how to operate it on at least a hundred different occasions, and it was only now that he wished he'd listened to him on at least one of them.

The nest was surrounded by technicians now, each dedicated to their own tasks, but synchronised like a ritual. Daytona stared through the camera at the scene before him, the record light flashing in the viewfinder like the wink of a demon. The dull grey eggs rattled against each other, their burnished surfaces slowly beginning to crack, hairline channels stretching out across the surface of the shells like dry rivers on an aerial map.

As the first broke open, it seemed as though everything in the compound halted for the briefest of moments - the technicians in their rehearsed confusion, the monitors with screens of ever-filling data - as the strongest of the engineered life-forms lurched from its shell and gulped its first lungfuls of processed oxygen.

Daytona began to feel light-headed as though the creature was drawing the very breath from his lungs. Its glistening flesh sparkled a rich deep scarlet, strands of amniotic fluid clinging to it like bile. As its mouth gaped to replace the fluid in its lungs with air, its needle-point spherical black eyes stared out through the glass at a world it could never recognise, and at its parents huddled around the crib who had struggled to bring it into such a world.

A second egg split apart and opened. And then a third. The technicians slowly began to overcome their bewilderment and record information on their computers. Daytona staggered blindly from the camera and stood amongst the technicians, his body coming between lens and subject. And as he peered in through the glass, the first infant looked up at him, its fingers reaching perhaps for his maternal breast, but he had no milk for it, only wonder. The second approached the glass, only to collapse, its neck twisting as its chest heaved and contorted. The first seemed to cope with the oxygen being pumped to it, more than cope, it seemed to thrive on it. It tried to stand on its legs and press itself to the glass like he, its red jacket tightening around growing muscle as it dried. The contact between his eyes and those of the alien child was such that he barely noticed the third drown in its own phlegm, choking as its lungs refused to give up what had nourished it since inception.

The rattling of the remaining three eggs calmed and then ceased altogether. From the nest of six, only one continued to breath.

A mixture of bodies from Genepool and Axis News burst into the room above the compound, the head of which rushed to the window to look down into the compound below, straining to see through the gaggle of technicians surrounding the nest.

"Shit," Kinard yelled. "It's already started."

"Open the door," Angel demanded. "We've got pictures to take."

Kinard turned and fell against the window. "I can't do that," he said, shaking his head dismally. "This door stays locked until the ELFs are secured."

Angel fished her phone from her pocket, punched in a few digits and waited. Looking down into the compound she saw Daytona, motionless and bent over, staring into the glass container.

"He's not answering," she said to the others. "Pick up the phone, Daytona, for God's sake."

Max joined her at the window.

"He's stood in front of the fucking camera," he said in despair.

She shook her head as she put her phone away and tried Kinard again.

"We've got to get down there," she said to him. "Emanuel wants pictures from us, and so far we've got Jack Shit.

The scarlet creature pressed its hands against the glass, pressed its face too, fogging the contact with condensation. The technicians were moving hurriedly now, but they were just an insignificant blur to Daytona. Only a few of their words did he comprehend, but their tone seemed agitated, worried even, as if they didn't know what to do with the data their instruments were receiving.

As he watched, it slowly occurred to him that the creature wasn't reaching for a maternal breast or for him. It was conscious of its imprisonment and scrutiny and was searching for escape. Though the glass was thick and the steel that bound it solid, Daytona faltered as he thought he saw a ripple pass out across the surface of the glass like a pebble cast into calm waters, its epicentre the creatures touch on the inside. He took a step backward, unsure even as he did so that his eyes weren't playing some kind of trickery upon him, but then there came a second ripple, then a third and a fourth, until the deep red flesh of the alien appeared as it pushed itself through the wall of the glass container and out into the air of the compound like a swimmer emerging from a pool.

The water closed behind it and it fell

tumbling to the floor, rising unharmed to scuttle beneath the maze of cables and computers. Daytona felt his legs give way as he watched it go, catching a brief splash of scarlet as it vanished before his head hit the ground.

"What the Hell's going on down there?" Angel cried, as she saw Daytona fall.

"I don't know," Kinard told her. "I... I can't see."

From above the compound all they could make out was a panic of lab technicians in white coats scrambling about the nest. Machines were being pushed aside, leads and wires wrenched out of connections; Kinard stared down helplessly, incredulous at what his people were doing. It just made no sense. In desperation, he pressed the intercom by the door.

"This is Kinard," he yelled. "What the fuck are you doing down there?"

He watched as one of the technicians below looked up, his flushed face rabid against the colour of his coat, and started towards the stairs. The scene in the compound had escalated into near frenzy as equipment everywhere was hauled aside, the floor strewn with a litter of read-outs and computer forms. The intercom buzzed as he reached the door, his words coming between heavy breaths.

"Mr Kinard, sir," he said, fighting for his breath. "The ELF... it... it escaped."

"Escaped? How in God's name did it get out."

"I don't know," he said. "The container... the glass just seemed to... to dissolve around it. One minute -"

"What about the others?"

"Others?"

"Yes, Kitchener, the other ELFs."

"Two expired, three didn't show."

Kinard cursed under his breath.

"We can't find the other one," Kitchener said. "What should we do?"

"What about our driver?" Angel called out over Kinard's shoulder. "What happened to him? Is he okay?"

"Find the ELF," Kinard yelled, ignoring the woman behind him. "Just find it and get it contained."

*   *   *

Hidden from view of the Explorer building, Jessie sat and waited for Kelso to emerge. His words had incited such curiosity in her that she now found herself hiding at the end of the road, desperate to know of his secrets; and secrets he had, that much she was aware of at least. She had to know who had the bone, or more importantly, where the eggs were that they had cloned from its DNA code. She had to stop them before it was too late; show them that there were lines of code so dangerous, so loaded with energy, that they were ultimately unfathomable. The other scientists must surely have found them too, she thought, drawing on yet another cigarette as she stared into the rear-view mirror. Or perhaps they didn't care - perhaps the promise of glory from such a discovery blinded them from the unknown or unknowable.

Anxiously she glanced at her watch. Four forty. Twenty minutes she'd been sat waiting. She was certain he hadn't left before her, and he had talked like he was going somewhere. If she had missed him...

She stabbed her cigarette out just as his black Mercedes sped past. Jessie looked up, startled, fumbling with the keys in the ignition as she watched it hurtle round a corner. Desperately outpaced, the white VW struggled to keep up with him, guessing turns when he disappeared from view. Dodging a truck at a junction, she found herself on a clear road, not a car in sight ahead of her. Angrily she punched the steering wheel, gazing out around her for any sign of salvation, but it was hopeless. Cursing herself, she slowed down and pulled off the road, and sat staring blankly ahead of her, frustrated that her trail had ended so quickly. Reaching down, she took up her cigarettes and lit one, the plume of smoke curling around her like a blue ball of cloud.

Jessie put the car into gear and pulled onto the road again. After maybe half a mile she passed the Genepool building on her right. Her heart pounded as she looked at it behind her in the mirror. Of course, she cursed her own stupidity, who else would have the resources for such advanced cloning. Swinging the car around against the flow of traffic, she sped back the way she had come, turning in towards the Genepool building. And there, parked at an angle in front of it, sat Kelso's shining black Mercedes.

*   *   *

"Tell me the worst," he demanded, finding Emanuel pacing a corridor.

"It's gone wrong," he whined. "It's all gone wrong."

"Where are the Orkhas?" Kelso wanted to know.

Emanuel looked up at him, his face knotted.

"The clones. Where are they?"

"There's just one," he told him, wiping his forehead with his hand. "It's down in the compound somewhere. Hell, it escaped the nest, who's to say it won't escape the compound. One of the news crew saw it -"

"What news crew?"

"I had them come in to record the entire event..."

His voice began to grow unsteady as the rage on Kelso's face heightened.

"You mean the whole world knows about this already?"

"I don't think so," Emanuel said, trembling. "I think they had a problem with the camera or something."

"I can only hope," he muttered under his breath.

"The technicians were crazy," Emanuel

continued. "Babbling about glass melting, how it fell through solid glass and steel -"

"But you don't know where it is now?" Kelso asked him.

"We had failsafes..," he mumbled, shaking his head.

Kelso turned and hurried away, leaving him to pace the corridor alone.

"There were bits of genetic code we didn't know..," Emanuel yelled out after him. "We didn't know... we just took what we needed..."

Hobart and Angel had managed to haul their driver up into a chair, a still body in the centre of the mayhem swirling around them. The door to the compound had been unlocked, the risk to security paling after accounts from various technicians of the past half hours insanity ranged from the unlikely to the absurd, and panic had set in just to find the creature. Nobody had even set eyes on it since it had fallen from the nest, and the concern was growing in furtive whispers that it was no longer inside the building.

"I think he's coming round," Angel said, as she put her hand to his brow, his eyes beginning to flicker open.

"What happened down here?" Hobart asked him.

"Search me," he replied, putting his hand to the back of his head. "Check the tape."

"Wish I could," Max said, appearing in front of him with the cracked shell of the camera. "The tape's no good, and this thing's totalled."

"I thought it was... it was reaching out for me..," Daytona said, staring blankly at them. "But it just wanted to be free."

"Don't we all," Angel returned, smiling.

Hobart went to question him further, but a woman suddenly appeared beside them, anxious to know what was going on.

"Where have you been for the last half hour?" he said to her incredulously. "One of the aliens escaped and nobody's seen it since."

"Nobody knows where it is?" she asked.

They shook their heads.

In stunned silence, they all watched her stagger away from them and wander further into the compound, clutching her head in confusion. Daytona dragged back their attention as he began again to mumble about the strange scarlet child.

Jessie made her way through the compound amid a gaggle of people in white coats and dark suits, bewildered by such confusion. Stepping cautiously between fallen instruments and scattered papers, she hoped no one would question her being there, and indeed they seemed more concerned with finding the creature that supplied their data rather than the data itself, and she passed through the door at the other end without attracting a single glance.

The boiler room was dark, the air thick and musty and tainted with diesel fumes, the pumps and generators humming contentedly to themselves. Stepping further into the gloom, her eyes slowly adjusting to enable her to find a path between the hulks of dull metal machinery, she became aware of a different tang in the air, an almost sweet taste like blossom. Certain that she was imagining it amid the stench of diesel, the further she walked the stronger it became, until its source showed itself to her.

Stepping round from behind one of the pumps, she came upon a delicate blue cloud, its body soft and luminescent, hanging in the air. Jessie approached hesitantly, gazing into its faint light, ethereal fingers drifting from its centre like ghosts. Somewhere behind her in the dark she heard the door close, the patter of blind footsteps slow and even as they entered and navigated the blackness. She looked deeper into the light blue ball of cloud, recalling that she only needed to look, and to touch, in order to understand. She had no microscope, she had no tape measure; all she had was her eyes and her hands, and before she was even aware of what she was doing, she was reaching out towards it.

The footsteps were growing louder behind her, but she was barely even conscious of them. The ghosts had started to wrap themselves around her fingers, snaking across her wrists and up over her arms. Closing her eyes, she took a step closer, the fingers reaching around her waist, caressing her as it pulled her into its embrace. Jessie let it take her, its touch as gentle as its light, her vision behind her closed eyelids radiant with the same blue glow, ebbing with its own delicate pulse.

The sound of the footsteps behind her faded in her consciousness, along with the drone of the pumps and the generators, and she was glad to be left alone inside the womb of light, its touch heavenly on her skin, as it took her completely into its embrace.

Part Two
Hanoi K'Baja

"You know of one world,
I know of two."

North

INSIDE THE CITY GATES

The telling of fables and fairy-tales has always involved the creation of fantastical places in which the characters could play out their parts; kings and princesses had towering castles to rule over; dragons had cloudless blue skies and jagged mountain peaks to soar between; and children had magical forests and gardens to explore. And if ever there was a story-teller who loved the beauty of such creation, then he must surely have stood where Jessie now found herself.

Standing on the treeline of a magnificent forest, she looked down over lush green pasture to a road thronging with travellers painted a myriad of dazzling colours. Ahead of her across the vast plains lay another carpet of forest, itself cloaking the base of a range of black mountains that stretched like a jagged crest across the horizon.

Jessie glanced behind her at the forest that had once been the dark boiler room of the Genepool building, the stench of diesel that had been so heavy in the air now replaced by the tang of pine carried to her on a balmy wind. Taking a few steps down the slope towards the road busy with travellers, she looked up at the bright cloudless sky, its sun white and warming above her. Having no idea of where she was she looked out again at the road and at the city that would be the end of so many peoples journeys. It was like no other she had ever seen, beautiful in the distance. With no point in staying amongst the trees of the forest, Jessie continued down the grassy bank towards the road, discerning more of the colourful travellers the nearer she went. At first she could make out that while most were on foot, some rode on the backs of beasts, and others in wagons laden with goods and possessions. But it was as she joined the throng that she realised her mistake in assuming that all the travellers were human.

Their origins, surely some born from fertile dreams, seemed too mystifying to comprehend. Even tongues she expected to at least be familiar; although most seemed to speak English, or colloquial dialects thereof, some were so strange and unintelligible that they sounded to her more like functions of the body rather than words of conversation. She found herself walking amongst a group who wore crests of flesh across their heads, and she wondered as she travelled just how much more of their bodies might be crested beneath their robes of gold and blue. Ahead of her were albinos with dreadlocks of white that fell as manes across their shoulders and back. And further on, walking tall and thin, were surely stick-men taken from a child's doodle; emaciated with limbs like stripped branches, teetering high over everyone else, their gaunt faces looking out over the masses. Even the beasts that some rode seemed stolen from some bizarre circus. While some rode horses, most preferred a larger mount, their backs bristled and their legs striped, their stubby heads set high atop long necks.

As the city drew nearer, the pace of the traffic began to slow. Jessie edged to the side of the road to see the bustling congestion outside the city gates. Many tents and shelters had been pitched around the gates, adding to the confusion, and she managed to squeeze through the crowds despite the many flocks of animals tethered together ready to be sold.

As she came close to the high gates, she noticed a tiny wooden rostrum decorated with painted cloths, a scrawny figure inside it leaning precariously over the edge. Resembling very little more than a domestic pig, his almost constant ranting was aimed towards whoever it was beneath him that she couldn't yet see, the staff in his hand flailing in all directions as if trying to batter flies. Easing through the crowd was both awkward and slow, but keeping her gaze fixed on the antagonising swine in his raised sty, she soon came within fifty yards of the gates. Now she could see who he was so abusively haranguing, and she was glad that she couldn't understand the language his obvious insults were in.

Jessie stood and watched as two of his officers carried out his instructions, pulling a handful of the crowd forward for him to see. As he pointed with his staff, so the officers searched the travellers, inside their robes or the trunks they were carrying, it didn't matter. Edging closer between the throng of spectators and those waiting in line, she saw the travellers offer up possessions and money, holding them forward in open hands. The pig-man looked at each offering in turn, pointing his staff in various directions as he ranted. She watched horrified as some were allowed to pass through into the city while others were beaten back into the crowd, their offerings taken regardless and cast into a vat at the base of the rostrum.

Jessie began to edge away as yet another handful approached from the crowd, eagerly waiting to be allowed into the great city, but no sooner had she turned to leave than a shout went up behind her. She glanced back, only to see the pig-man pointing his staff at somebody in the crowd. Following his attention, she noticed the two officers rush from the gates - a monumental mistake. No sooner had they reached the edge of the crowd and begin their pursuit, than the remainder of the crowd surged forward towards the unguarded entrance. Caught up in the panic, Jessie found herself taken from her feet and bustled back as if dragged by a riptide. She only had time to see the pig in his decorated sty hurl his staff into the masses in desperation before she was swept through the open gates and on into the city.

The thronging surge began to disperse as

the gates inevitably closed, every illegal traveller seeming to push their way into the same narrow street and plaza to conceal their escape. Jessie ran behind a family of white dreadlocks, their efforts hampered by two small children failing to keep up. She passed them and ducked into a side-street as one of the parents turned to pick up the slowest of them.

Running to the end of the street, she emerged exhausted at a congested marketplace, and fell against a wall as she fought to get her breath back. She glanced down the narrow street behind her and was thankful that nobody had followed her. Taking a crumpled pack of cigarettes from her jacket pocket, she lit one and inhaled deeply before setting off into the busy market.

The dirt streets were jammed with the same menagerie of pedestrians as the road to the city. She still saw many that were human, as well as the dreadlocks and towering stick-men, but there were also new breeds to be seen, each as vividly coloured and intriguing as the next. Passing through the crowds were the same pig-like officers from the gate, the swell of shoppers and vendors parting to allow them through unhindered, but they paid little or no attention to her or indeed to any possible illegal entrant. Stray dogs and children ran between legs, stolen food clasped between teeth and unwashed fingers, the occasional shout rising up from behind them.

As Jessie came to the edge of the market and looked back at the bustling crowd, a short man appeared beside her, pulling at his long beard as he looked up at her.

"You look lost, child," he said, his voice as thin as the hair on his head. "New in the city, are you?"

"Where am I?" Jessie asked him.

"Why, you're in the city of Hanoi k'Baja, of course," he replied, grinning.

Jessie was about to tell him that didn't help, when he took hold of her hand and began to lead her away from the market.

"Where are we going?"

"Someplace safe," he told her. "Unless you'd prefer to stay on the streets."

Jessie looked over her shoulder at the people bustling about their lives, and the officers patrolling the unfriendly streets. An invitation to safety seemed too good to pass up; at least until she worked out where on earth she was.

"My name's Cat Cattah," he told her, as they walked. "I'm taking you to my house. There're others there who were lost in the city like you."

"You told me the name of the city," she said to him, "but where exactly is the city."

"You're more lost than I thought," he chuckled.

They turned into a side-street between two tenement buildings, the floor littered with debris, small creatures burrowing unseen beneath boxes and sacks. The stench of rot and stale urine was overwhelming as the two of them stirred up the foul dirt with their feet.

"Are you alone?" Cat asked her, as they emerged into another more wider street. "No one to come after you?"

"Not here," she said.

"Run away from home?"

"I didn't run exactly..."

He told her that he understood as they took a left, tall housing blocks on either side of them now. About halfway down the street, Cat stopped and ushered her up some steps to a door, and said:

"Here we are. My house; home to the city's lost."

It was dark inside, and there was a sickly stench of tobacco and alcohol in the warm air. The old man hurried her through and into a small kitchen out back, calling out to somebody elsewhere in the house as they went.

"I'll see if I can find her," he explained irritably. "She can be a little lazy when it's late in the day. Please help yourself to whatever you can find."

Once he had disappeared back into the house, Jessie began to wander around the tiny kitchen, peering into the jars and clay pots stacked on shelves. A small window was set in one of the walls, looking out on the side of the neighbouring building less than an arms reach away. Taking up one of the jars, she peered inside at what looked to be strips of dried meat. Jessie sniffed at them cautiously before taking a bite. The meat was hard and tough, her teeth barely making an impression in its dark hide. Replacing the strip she took up another jar and found oval biscuits, and in another blue berries. The biscuits were bland and dry, the fruit welcome afterwards with its sweet juice. Drinking from a bottle she found in one of the cupboards, she didn't hear Cat Cattah return to the kitchen behind her. Jessie turned to see him with a young girl whose skin fluttered around her like silken veils, rainbows of exquisite iridescent colours rippling inside them in shimmering waves, her nakedness fleeting beneath such translucency. Her face was long and beautiful, yet her eyes were sad and stayed at the floor.

"This is Ula Mia'h," Cat said to her. "She will show you to your room. If there's anything you need, just ask her."

Jessie thanked him as she wiped the juice from her lips and put the bottle back in the cupboard. Cat stayed in the kitchen as she followed the girl of veils back into the dark and odorous house, before being taken up a flight of stairs and along a corridor. There were maybe half a dozen doors along the dimly lit passage, and Ula Mia'h led her to the one at the very end. Her eyes still cast to the floor, she waited until Jessie crossed the threshold. The tiny room was poorly furnished, a single candle on a table next to the bed, a washbowl in the corner, and very little else.

"What is this place?" Jessie asked, as she went to the shuttered window.

"It is a place where the homeless find a home," Ula replied quietly.

"How long have you been here?" she asked her, attempting to open the shutters.

"I can't remember a time before I was here. This is all I know."

Jessie gave up on the locked shutters and looked back at the sad but beautiful girl hovering in the doorway. She had not seen her eyes, but now they looked up at her, glistening with tears as she said:

"I pray you do not stay long."

Jessie went to tell her that it was only for a day or so, but the girl had already gone.

2

Built on the banks of the River Suracoa, Hanoi k'Baja had grown quickly from a fishing port to a city. Too quickly, some had said, for decent development. Temporary tenements had become permanent as the sprawl grew like an uncontrollable infection, unable to be treated properly as travellers and gypsies arrived daily into the harbour and at the city gates from as far north as the tropics of Kwitala, as far west as the deserts of Aran, and as far south as the coastal regions of Pal'Alata.

As the city grew however, a government

appointed itself from the richest of the port merchants, and it was soon decided that enough was enough. A high city wall was built and soldiers drafted to police it. Nomads still arrived daily and shanty towns began to build up outside the wall, and violence and crime inevitably escalated amongst the most desperate of the multi-racial community. Only a small proportion of those were allowed into the city, if they had sufficient monies to support themselves or at the discretion of the police. The merchants' policy was a good one. It was the execution by the ill-trained and mercenary police that destroyed it. But the merchants had their own businesses to spend their hours with, and so the corruption, much like the welfare of the populace, was gravely overlooked and ignored.

On the edge of the harbour in one of the first tenement buildings to be built, a secret meeting of the Bening Tai'Orkha was close to breaking down. With the windows heavily shuttered against the day, the council of twelve sat in heated debate.

"I can see no reason why this should not be our last meeting," Mai Turk said yet again, kicking his chair back to pace the room.

"We can never give up hope," retorted Ash Ahee. "Some of our agents still have not returned -"

"And nor will they return," Mai slammed his fists on the table in front of her. "They are dead, murdered by Depurates."

"I can not believe -"

"You can not accept," he stormed, "that there are only a few remaining Orkhas left in the Jume."

"I'm afraid I have to agree with you," said Llumi d'Ha solemnly. "As much as it pains us all, we all knew this day would come. I fear we can do no more."

"But surely you're not suggesting that we simply let what few spirits remain be slaughtered like the rest?" Ash Ahee was incredulous.

"I don't see that it makes any difference now."

"But Llumi -"

"The dead will never find Natura on their own. They will simply be lost."

*   *   *

119

3

Amongst the fishing boats tied up in the harbour bobbed an old trawler, its deck full of cases of rotting fish and knotted nets. Below deck, behind portholes blackened with algae, two men argued with another customer.

"And I tell you the price has gone up," said the boat owner. "Yes, again."

"Listen to me, Cohoka, we agreed on a price. I wouldn't wipe my arse with filth like you, but this is business and I have little choice."

"Your ethics serve you well, Bruun, but there are other buyers who will pay what I ask."

The buyer leapt to his feet as he reached for the man's throat, but his head connected with the boats low ceiling before he could touch him and he reeled back in pain.

"Maybe we could do a deal," suggested M'Lyon Saak, who had not spoken for a while.

"We did a deal," snapped Bruun, clutching his head.

"You're a good customer," said Saak. "Let's say only an extra ten instead of thirty."

Bruun's lips grew thin.

"Five," he said, through gritted teeth.

"Seven," Cohoka countered.

"Okay," he conceded, and reluctantly took Saak's outstretched hand.

The two men exchanged furtive grins as Bruun reached into his long coat and took out a bag of coins. As he began to count, there came a thud of footsteps across the deck above them. Pushing the bag back into his coat as the footsteps hammered down the steps towards them, the two smugglers barely had time to reach for their weapons before the door to the galley flew off its hinges, the lock splintering the wooden frame.

The two men stared open-mouthed at the man standing in the broken doorway. A wide grin was on his face. And then one of them stammered:

"Master."

TWO

THE SICKENING TRUTH

The only light in the street below spilled from Cat Cattah's open doorway. Through the slats of the locked window shutters Jessie had seen a number of people shuffle inside, the drone of their voices still echoing up from the rooms below. It couldn't have been long after the first of the arrivals that there came a light knock at her door. Jessie called out for them to come in, and standing there in the doorway stood Ula Mia'h, radiant within her rainbow silks of skin. Seeming not to enjoy her beauty, her eyes still cast downward, she approached carrying a fine silken robe in her arms, which she held forward for Jessie to take.

"Cat would prefer you to wear this," she said softly.

Jessie held it up in front of her. It was indeed a most beautiful cloth, a weave of the finest and lightest threads, but through it she could see the unhappy girl of veils. She thanked her but knew that there was no way she could wear it without exposing herself beneath, and told Ula that Cat would just have to get used to seeing her in what she was already wearing.

"I also brought this for you," she told Jessie, handing her a small bottle.

"What is it?" she asked.

"It's called batka. It helps to numb your thoughts."

"Back home we settle for whiskey and dope," she smiled, uncorking the bottle. After sniffing at it she took a sip of the potent liquor. "What is this?" she spluttered, as it began to burn at her throat.

"It heals pain," Ula said, turning to leave. "And memories."

Jessie recorked the bottle and put it on the table, the fire in her throat bringing tears to her eyes. Looking up, she saw Ula hovering at the doorway.

"Please, I beg you, drink from the bottle," she whispered, and then she went, closing the door behind her.

Jessie wasn't sure what pain the batka could heal, but she was certain it would be preferable to the pain of actually drinking it. She looked down at the fine robe Ula had brought for her, and felt its silken texture between her fingers again. Then turning her back on it, she left the room and stepped out into the empty corridor. The air was tainted with the raucous conversation and laughter that drifted up from the rooms below, along with the fresh stench of tobacco and alcohol. There also came an inane tune played on some kind of tinny piano, a totally unmusical dirge that must surely have been irritating to those downstairs at the very least.

As she passed one of the doors on her right, she noticed the grunt and wheeze of what sounded like a large dog busy at its dinner, although she had not noticed there being a dog in the house earlier. She continued towards the stairs, leaving it to its appetite, the smoke from downstairs now rising visibly in light blue plumes. She could see nothing from the top of the stairs as she peered down, and so cautiously she began to descend.

Jessie had maybe gone halfway when she bent to look through the railings, and then the dawning of Cat's home to the lost, the transparent robe and the batka suddenly hit her like a punch in the gut. Sitting on one of the padded suites was Ula, a grotesquely fat creature beside her, his bulbous hands beneath her rainbow veils and between her legs. What Jessie could see of his head that wasn't buried salivating at her neck, was slick with grease, long flaps hanging like chins down his neck and back. His belly fell across Ula's thigh as he worked his hands, yet not once did she push the beast away. Jessie held back a sob as she looked at the beautiful girl of veils, realising now why she took the batka, her eyes no longer cast downward but stoned and empty, and it was all she could do not to cry out for her. She noticed maybe three or four more of Cat's customers engrossed in similar molestation as she turned away to hurry back up the stairs.

Running now along the corridor, she passed the door behind which she thought a dog had been at its supper. Halting mid-stride, she returned to it, putting her ear to the door. Still the creature barked and wheezed, only now she could hear the creak of wood and the slap of flesh on flesh. Her mind picturing the sickening scene on the other side of the door, Jessie burst into the room before she had time to think.

From the dim glow of a candle each side of the bed, she could see the confusion of bodies entwined, naked and sweating. Jessie made out the same stoned expression of the girl on her back as she snatched up one of the candles. The eyes of the creature pumping away on top flickered open briefly, before Jessie pushed its flame into his dark fleshy buttocks. His grunts of effort turned instantly to howls of pain as his rump blistered from fire and burning wax. Scrambling from the open legs beneath him, the molten wax running down to burn his balls, he reached to take up his clothes from the floor to cover himself, but by the light of the remaining candle she could see the agony had brought water to his eyes and a droop to his failing erection.

Jessie scrambled after him, leaping across the bed, her fingers seeking to tear at his flesh. The creature stumbled back, hitting the wall hard before collapsing into the corner of the room. Desperately her hands sought out weapons, her fingers falling upon his discarded belt, its buckle large and heavy. Her eyes blinded with rage now, she followed the whimpering ahead of her, and swung the belt after it as hard as she could. The buckle whistled through the air as it missed its target, but conjured a yelp of fear which made her teeth grin.

She hadn't heard the laughter or conversation die to a whisper since she had stormed into the room, but now she heard the thunder of footsteps on the stairs and in the passage outside. Her senses told her to run, but the need to give pain overtook her, and she found herself raising the belt above her head again.

The second swing came as the creature tried to duck, but the buckle connected, its metal tasting blood as the skin broke under the impact. His hand went to the wound as she lashed out again, the bone of his skull cracking now, and again with the fourth. The fifth contact brought a wet sound like fruit falling on tiles, and panting she let the belt fall to the ground, turning to see a number of people rush to the doorway behind her.

Jessie glanced at the young girl on the bed who had not moved, her legs still open and glistening with sweat, as she circled the bed, running headlong at the door. Such was the surprise of the handful of people huddled in the passage that she managed to burst through untouched and out towards the stairs. Ignoring the shouts rising up behind her, she hurried blindly down to the room below, her feet missing steps as she went, grabbing hold of the bannisters to keep her upright. Stumbling now, she caught sight of the open doorway and the darkened street outside through a haze of confusion, yet they were taken from her as she felt a blow to her side that sent her reeling to the floor. Trying to shake the dizziness from her senses, she hauled herself to her feet to see Cat Cattah hurrying down the stairs towards her. She looked round to get her bearings and make for the door, but she had hardly taken a step before she felt an arm around her throat and another at her back, holding her still.

"What is this you do to me, bitch?" Cat raged as he reached her, bringing the back of his hand hard across her face, stinging her cheek with pain. "I give you my house to live in, my food to put in your belly, and this is how you repay me."

"You fuck," was all she could spit, the taste of her blood on her tongue, as she struggled in vain against the hold behind her.

"I should have left you on the street," he

hissed. "Better yet, I'll have all my customers fuck you for free, then I'll dump your body in the Suracoa."

As Cat Cattah raised his hand again to strike her, a gun shot rang out, and the man holding Jessie loosened his grip before sliding dead to the floor. Jessie stumbled back as he fell, looking round at her saviour standing in the open doorway, as too did Cat.

"Let her go," the young man called to him, aiming his revolver into the room.

"Luke?" she stammered. "Luke, is that you?"

"It's me," he replied. "Come to me quickly."

Jessie hurried away from Cat and the man dead at her feet. She paused halfway to glance back at Ula Mia'h. She had not moved from the padded suite, her expression still stoned and empty. Jessie did not want to leave her but she knew she had very little choice, and continued to Luke's side.

"We will meet again," Cat said bitterly as they went to leave. "I'm owed more favours in this city than anyone else, believe me."

"Empty threats," Luke retorted. "You'll never find us."

"Oh, I'll find you," Cat returned. "No

matter where you hide, I'll find you."

Stepping out through the open doorway, his revolver still trained on the short old man, they turned and headed into the night, hoping they would not be followed and that the dark streets would shroud their escape.

Everything was dark except for the meagre light that spilled from shuttered windows or cracks between doors, the light from the stars overhead unable to penetrate sufficiently between the tall tenement buildings constructed so close together for them to see by. They passed nobody as they hurried through the maze of passageways, the streets surprisingly quiet after the crowds so busy beneath daylight.

"Can we stop soon?" Jessie panted.

"I want to get out of the streets," he said to her. "I think we're nearly at the harbour. We can rest there."

Another narrow passageway led them into an open plaza. After picking one of the routes out of it, they eventually ended up outside the city buildings and standing at the top of a grassy slope, a vast harbour spread out below, lights sparkling in the windows of the fishing boats as they bobbed at the quay.

Jessie and Luke wandered down the slope a little way before stopping to rest. Despite there being no moon, the light from the countless stars illuminated the scene before them, bringing surreal beauty to it all. Looking down from the hill past the harbour, the waters of the river glittered with the reflections of the endless galaxies and constellations above, the banks and plains beyond radiant as if glowing with their own incandescence. Jessie lay back on her elbows, sighing as she stared up at the beautiful night sky.

"It's a shame we started our tour in such a rotten part of the city," Luke said to her.

"I still haven't thanked you," she told him. "You seem to be making a habit of saving my skin."

"It's a beautiful skin to save."

Jessie looked round at him, but he had turned away.

"Tell me again why you're here," she asked him.

"North said that the questions you were asking were going to get you into trouble."

"He wasn't wrong," she said.

"He told me to follow you. Make sure no harm came to you."

"Even under Ashen Bridge?"

"No, that was luck," he said, looking at her and smiling.

Jessie held his gaze this time, staring at his young face. His eyes glittered like the river below them, the cool night air ruffling his hair. But too soon he looked away again, back to the harbour at the bottom of the slope.

"We shouldn't stay out in the open too long," he said, getting to his feet.

"No," she agreed, taking his hand.

"We'll carry on down into the harbour."

"Are we going someplace special?" she asked him.

Luke reached into his jacket pocket and pulled out a crumpled sheet of paper. As he tried to smooth it out Jessie looked at it over his shoulder, and at the marks and lines scrawled upon it.

"North drew me a map..." Luke told her.

"A map?" she stammered. "How could he possibly draw you a map. Unless..." she looked at Luke but he remained silent. "He's been here before? What is this? Does everyone know where I am except me?"

"No, no. If this is Hanoi k'Baja, then North knew this place pretty well. Although..." he

132

said, staring at the map.

"Although, what?"

"This map shows a small port on a river, see?" he showed her. "And it's a damn sight smaller than the city we're in."

"So what are you telling me?" Jessie wanted to know.

"I'm telling you that he only gave me one address."

They continued down the hill in silence, Jessie thinking to herself how both Hassan and North had almost spoken in riddles when she'd asked them her questions. Now she knew how naive those questions must have seemed to someone who knew of other worlds, other dominions. It must have seemed like a deaf person asking to have music explained to them by a composer - it would have been overwhelming to the point of absurdity.

Towards the bottom of the hill they came upon the first of the old port buildings, constructed with imagination and care, so different to those thrown up in the new city behind them. She saw Luke take the map from his pocket again, and hold it close to his face to see, but it was much darker here, the buildings shielding much of the light from the stars. He looked up when he noticed her watching him curiously, an embarrassed smile on his lips.

"No torch?" she asked him.

"No torch," he said, shaking his head. "I didn't think..."

Jessie fished into her jacket and pulled out her cigarette lighter.

"It's a bad habit, I know," she said, smiling as she handed it to him.

Standing beside him, she watched as he cast its tiny flame across the crumpled sheet. There was not much written on it, just a handful of black jagged lines and a few words, place names she guessed.

"So where are we headed?" she asked him.

Luke ran his finger along one of the lines for her to see.

"This street here," he said, "should lead us to the Order of the Bening Tai'Orkha."

"Which is..?"

"Which is about the only place North told me about."

"Great," she said, putting her hands on her hips. "And if we don't find this place, or the map's wrong, or anything else - what do we do then?"

Luke shrugged. It was obvious to her that

134

he was fully aware of their dilemma.

"Why the hell would you want to follow me here?" she wanted to know.

"It was all I had to be close to you," he told her, looking away as he gave her back her lighter, before putting the map back in his pocket.

Jessie softened a little.

"I don't know, Luke," she said. "I don't know whether to hate myself for coming here, or you for following."

He looked back at her guiltily.

"I'm just joking. I'm glad you're here," she said. "Now where's this address."

They started out into the old port buildings, travelling along North's jagged line as best they could. According to the map, it wasn't far away, but more than once they came upon an junction that wasn't on the map, and they continued blindly. Luke stopped as they came to yet another junction, where he stood and looked up at a two storey building.

"I think this is it," he murmured.

"Are you sure?"

"No," he said, and stepped towards the door.

Jessie stayed in the street and stared up at

the stars still bright and sparkling in the coal black sky. Astrology had been Larson's passion since she had first met him all those years ago. He had wanted to share his passion, showing her star charts and constellation patterns countless times. It disillusioned him on occasion when she told him she thought they just looked pretty. And staring up at the sky now, she still thought that.

Luke approached the door, nervous as a thief. He wasn't sure what he was going to say to these people, despite the frequent times he had planned it in his head, so that it wouldn't sound like the ramblings of an insane drunk. He felt sure he wouldn't get away with what North had told him to say. As he went to knock on the door, he caught sight of lights flickering inside the building through the grill. Putting his ear to the door, he could make out urgent whispering and the shuffling of feet.

Tentatively he rapped lightly, the sound echoing out in the silence of the night. The whispering and shuffling stopped instantly, and the light he had seen inside the building flickered out. Again he rapped at the door and asked this time if anyone was there. He waited a few moments, and then he heard the shuffling feet approach the door at speed, the grill opening a crack. A middle-aged face appeared, half-hidden by shadow and door timber. Luke tried to discern some of the man's features but it was darker inside than out.

"What do you want?" the face hissed.

"Is this the Order of the Bening Tai'Orkha?"

"It is."

"I was told to ask for your help, and that I might ask for shelter tonight."

"Oh, you were, were you?" the face was intrigued. "Are you a member of the Order?"

"No, but -"

"Then fuck off," he said, and slammed shut the grill.

Luke stared at the door for a moment and listened to the footsteps hurry away back into the building. The whispering started up again, only this time more urgent and insistent. North had told Luke that the Order had its secrets to keep, but he didn't feel quite so sure. He thought that perhaps he should have told him who had sent him, but would they even remember anything that had happened over twenty years ago, and would it matter at all to the man behind the grill. Still, he thought, it had waited two decades already, another day wouldn't hurt. One thing he was sure about, though, was that they were not getting in tonight.

Leaving the doorway he turned to tell Jessie the news and saw her standing in the middle of the road staring up at the sky. He wanted to go and tell her that they would have to sleep somewhere else, but his feet wouldn't move. He just stood and looked at her, tranquil and beautiful.

"Everything alright?" she asked him, when he at last joined her.

"Perfect," he whispered, his eyes still entranced.

THREE

ANOTHER DAY WOULDN'T HURT

Blinds drawn against the sun, Victor Emanuel sat in his office staring into space. He hadn't moved all morning and had refused all calls. Outside in the corridor he could hear a heated argument, and then the door to his office burst open and Kinard stood struggling with his secretary. Finally pushing her to one side, he approached the man slumped in his chair, the woman looking apologetically at Emanuel, who waved her back to her desk.

"What the fuck are you sitting in here for?" Kinard yelled, slamming his fists on his desk sending papers flying. "It's all I can do to keep order down there."

Emanuel ran his trembling hands through his hair.

"I don't know what to do," he said quietly.

"I'll tell you what you do," Kinard told him. "You get the fuck out of this office, go downstairs, and sort this fucking shit out."

"I don't know what to do," he said again in despair. "I really don't."

Kinard stormed round to the other side of the desk and hauled Emanuel to his feet.

"For a start, what do we do about the five ELF corpses?" he wanted to know.

Emanuel stared blankly at him, helpless beneath his grasp.

"Do we incinerate them or what?"

"I guess so," he said feebly.

Kinard sighed in disgust and then dropped him back into his chair. Storming from his office, he hurried back through the Genepool building to the observation room overlooking the compound, grabbing the first two technicians he came to.

"I want you to stop whatever you're doing and go to the cryogenic chamber -"

"But we're supposed to be checking data," one of them said.

"Fuck the data," he yelled, losing his patience. "Go to the cryogenic chamber and take the ELFs to the incinerator."

"Incinerator?"

"Yes, the incinerator. What, it's got too many syllables in it? Now get the ELFs and burn the fuckers. I want nothing left."

The two technicians nodded hesitantly and started away, but as Kinard looked down into the compound below he suddenly stopped them.

"Where's Highwater?" he asked them.

They looked at him blankly.

"Highwater?" he shouted. "Where the fuck is Highwater?"

The man appeared at the door looking bemused.

"What's the problem?" he asked as he approached.

"Who's that down there?" Kinard asked him, pointing to a man down in the compound examining the remains of the nest.

"He said that Emanuel had sent for him. That he was authorised to be down there."

"And you call yourself security?" he said, leaving him and hurrying down the steps into the compound. Grabbing the intruder by the shoulder, he spun him round and said:

"Who the fuck are you?"

"Mr Emanuel wanted to -"

"Bullshit," Kinard raged. "Emanuel wants nothing. He's up in his office pissing in his pants. Now tell me who you really are before I have your legs broken."

"Okay, okay. My name is Robert Larson. I'm from the Explorer facility -"

"Another one? There was a guy here earlier from Explorer. Haven't seen him since."

"Well, I had to see for myself."

"See what?" Kinard eyed him curiously.

"The creatures you cloned," he said. "I had to see them."

"What creatures? I don't know what you're talking about."

"There's nothing to cover up. I know all about the bone. It was me who first discovered it." Kinard went to grab him but he fended it off. "I was head of a space program. The probe brought the bone back with it. We thought it had been destroyed along with the lab, when all along you'd had it stolen."

"We didn't steal anything," Kinard said, his words trailing weakly. "Emanuel said -"

"Where else would you get such a bone? Not from this world."

Kinard's mind was racing now.

"I don't know..." he stammered. "I never

asked... never thought..."

"You never cared, that was the difference," Larson said to him. "You were so keen for the rewards that you didn't wait to do all the work."

"We did what we could -"

"But you didn't do it all."

Kinard stumbled backward, clutching his head in confusion, both his strength and his words now draining from his body.

"Where are the creatures now?"

Kinard looked up at him with empty eyes.

"The creatures, where are they?

"There were six," he started, trying to shake the haze from his head. "Five died."

"And the sixth?"

"We lost it. It... it escaped somehow. There was no trace..."

"Maybe with the other five we could continue to research..." Larson's words trailed off as he saw Kinard's expression drop from his face.

Luke woke from his bed of old nets as something brushed past his face. Swiping it away, he opened his eyes to see a small figure darting furtively around them. Spinning round, he reached out to grab hold of the thief but his fingers touched only air, the elusive figure leaping up and away, scrambling to the top of a high wall above them. Jessie woke as Luke leapt to his feet in pursuit, the thief hopelessly out of reach, and he sat smiling down at him as he glanced over what he had taken.

"Give me that back," Luke yelled up at the young boy, his white dreadlocks falling down across his shoulders like a mane, as he opened up the map and surveyed it.

"Give it back," he yelled again, desperately trying to reach up to snatch it back.

"What do you want it for?" the boy asked plainly.

"We have to find our way back to the Order of the Orkha," Jessie said, getting to her feet.

"That'll be difficult with this map."

"And why's that?" Luke snapped. "We used it last night."

"Oh, the Order's on here," the dreadlock boy said. "But Ayella's Boatyard isn't."

"And what's that?"

"You're standing on it."

Luke looked at Jessie whose face echoed his frustration.

"But if you like," the boy said, dropping the map down to them, "I'll take you there."

"No thanks," Luke muttered, irritably. "We found it once, we can find it again."

"Suit yourself," he retorted, and disappeared over the wall.

"Luke," Jessie said, grabbing his arm. "What are you doing? He said he'd take us there."

"How can we trust him? He just stole from us, remember? He lives on the streets."

"So do you," Jessie reminded him. "I thought you could have shown him a little compassion."

"I think I read him pretty well," he remarked, tucking the map away in his jacket. "He's only out for himself. He'd probably lead us somewhere and then slit our throats."

"Well I think you're wrong," Jessie said, walking past him.

Once they left the boatyard, it surprised them both how different the streets looked now they could see them in daylight. They walked for what seemed like an age up and down rows of timber buildings and huts, both cursing their rashness with the dreadlock child. It made both of them feel guilty; Luke for not trusting his own kind, even though he still felt sure he had been right, and Jessie for not stepping in at the time. And as a result they mostly travelled in silence.

"I think this may be it," Luke said, as they arrived at another junction.

"You've said that several times already," Jessie remarked, testily.

"It's at the bottom of the hill."

"You've said that as well."

"How long are you going to keep this up?" he asked her, coming to a halt.

"Keep what up, exactly?"

"You want an apology, is that it?"

Jessie raised an eyebrow but remained silent.

"Okay, so I was a bit hasty back there. I'm sorry."

"And?"

Luke hung his head and sighed.

"I felt like I had a purpose at last," he said. "North sending me after you. I guess I got a little full of myself. I know I'm still a nothing on the street -"

"Hey," Jessie said, touching his arm. "You're not a nothing."

"But I am on the street."

"So am I," she said, smiling at him.

"It's different," he told her. "*You're* different."

"I don't have a home anymore. Or a job. There's nobody to take care of me; no husband, no family. I have to look out for myself. Believe me, we're not as different as you think."

Luke went to say something, but paused and then stayed quiet. He looked round at the junction once more and told her again that he thought they were in the right place. Approaching the door of the building on the corner, they noticed that it was standing ajar. They looked at one another before Luke rapped lightly on the door jamb. They waited a moment but there was no answer.

"Maybe we should go in," Jessie suggested, pushing the door open to see inside.

"I don't want to run into that man again."

"What man?" she asked, but he was already over the threshold.

The hallway was chilly and quiet, not a sound coming from anywhere in the building apart from their own footsteps on the wooden floor. They continued to call as they went, but still no one answered. The hall led to a flight of steps that went up, and after peering up started to ascend. A warm current of air came down from the floor above - someone had presumably left a window open as well as the door - and it carried a strong yet sweet taste upon it that grew more pungent as they climbed. They discovered the source of the sickly stench as they reached the top of the stairs.

Awash with blackened blood, the timbered floor made like an abattoir; carcasses lying with throats slit, limbs of meat hacked and battered, racks of ribs cracked and opened up; a fine feast for the black hum of flies eager at the wet flesh.

Jessie stumbled amongst the slaughter to the open window, leaning out to where the air was untainted. Luke stayed at the stairs, his eyes shut against the sight, holding onto the bannister with white knuckles to keep him standing. With several breaths of clean air inside her lungs, Jessie turned back shuddering.

"This was the Order?" she stammered.

Luke trembled as he nodded, his eyes still clenched.

"Who would do something like this?" she said.

"You already know," came a voice behind her.

Jessie spun round to see the dreadlock child

perched on the window sill.

"You saw him last night," the boy said to Luke, who had opened his eyes now he had been addressed. "You saw the face of the Order's enemy; the face of the Depurate."

"How do you know -"

"You disturbed them as they stood over their beds."

"I disturbed them?" Luke said. "You mean I could have saved them?"

"Perhaps, perhaps not," the boy said, shrugging. "Now it can only be speculation."

Luke hung his head and closed his eyes again, rubbing at his hair with his hands.

"You weren't to know," Jessie said to him, and turning to the boy at the window, added, "If what you say is true -"

"Why would I lie?" he said, his face angelic.

"If you were here, then why didn't you try and stop them?"

The dreadlock child said nothing, but simply smiled at her and cocked his head to one side. Jessie lost her temper and grabbed hold of him. The boy lost his balance as he went back, snatching at her wrist and hanging on to it desperately.

"Hey, it wasn't me holding the knife," he

protested, trying to wrestle his weight back onto the sill.

"You may as well have been," she retorted. "Perhaps you deserve the same."

Luke was by her side now, trying to calm her.

"Don't you think this place has seen enough blood," he said.

Jessie sighed and let go of her grip.

"Besides," the boy continued, glad to have his balance back, "not all of the Order died here last night."

Jessie moved to grab him again, but he backed away as much as he could on the sill, and avoided her grasp.

"One of them fell from this window during the frenzy. A young man. He must've busted himself up, because I watched him crawl away from the street. He didn't look good."

"Did you follow him?"

"Of course I followed him."

"Then take us to him," Jessie demanded.

"In return for what?"

Jessie moved to grab him again and this time she caught hold of his shirt and held him off-balance out of the window, his arms flailing for support.

"Take us," she said. "Or you'll be taking the same route he did."

FOUR

ONE DOOR CLOSES, ANOTHER OPENS

Outside the Axis News building a grey BMW screeched to a halt. Robert Larson dragged Kinard from the car, hauling him up the steps and into the building. After clearing them with the news crew, the security guard gave them directions to the third floor where Angel stood impatiently waiting to meet them.

"Just what the hell is going on with you lot?" she asked Kinard, as soon as he emerged from the elevator. "First you want us to record your greatest moment, then you kick us out and refuse all phonecalls."

"The truth is -"

"The truth is," Larson interrupted, "they fucked up."

"And who might you be?" she wanted to

152

know.

"My name is Robert Larson. I work for Explorer."

"I remember," she said, as they started down the corridor. "Bomb blast a few months back. Natural rights group, wasn't it?"

"It might have been better if it was," he told her. "But Genepool destroyed the labs to cover up one of my finds they wanted -"

"One of *your* finds?"

"I didn't come here to give you an update for your six o'clock bulletin," Larson told her impatiently. "I came here to see the film you shot of the creatures."

"Then I'm afraid you've had a wasted journey," Angel said, as they arrived at the control room door. "Most of it is no good. Our driver got in the way of the lens and then he smashed the camera."

"What's he like at driving?" Larson remarked, as they went in.

Angel took them over to a man sat at a board of equipment in front of a number of monitors. The man, whom she introduced as Max, plugged in a video cassette, the monitors sparking a snowstorm that faded into a view of the compound at Genepool.

"I'm afraid it watches like a cheap B-movie," Angel told them, shaking her head. "We caught hardly any of the hatching. You can see something moving behind his body," she pointed at one of the screens, "scraps of red, but nothing more."

From behind the body obscuring much of the screen, they could make out the technicians huddled over bits of equipment, making notes and recording data. But then the scene seemed to break into pandemonium, the same calm technicians now darting in panic and confusion. The body in front of the camera started to stagger backwards, the room spiralled as it fell, and then the screen went black.

"That's it," Angel said, ejecting the tape.

Larson slumped against the wall and sighed in frustration.

"So where do we go from here?" she asked them both.

"Search me," Larson told her. "The only person who knows anything about these things is missing."

"And who might that be?"

"The first person to start researching their DNA. Jessica McHard."

"Doesn't ring any bells," Angel said,

shaking her head. "Did she tell you anything useful the last time you saw her?"

"She said a lot of things," he told her. "She was really angry. And confused. She might have done anything."

"Did she mention any names, any places?"

"No, only about the research," Larson said, shaking his head. "Except she had talked about a man I'd never heard of before any of this started."

"And who was that?"

"I think he was a vagrant - lived on the street. It might only be a coincidence..."

"There's no such thing," Angel pointed out. "Can you remember his name?"

Larson closed his eyes as he searched his memory; the man hadn't seemed important at the time.

"North," he said at last. "I think it was North."

"No," Angel said, shaking her head slowly. "Doesn't ring any bells either. But at least it's a start."

The door to the small control opened and a man strolled in carrying a Styrofoam cup of coffee. Angel got to her feet as he approached.

"Hobart," she said to him. "Have you heard

of a researcher called Jessica McHard?"

The man shook his head as he stirred his coffee.

"How about a vagrant called North?"

Hobart narrowed his eyes as he took a couple of sips.

"We did a piece on the homeless in Hartwell a little while back," he said. "I think one of them was called North."

"Are you sure?"

"Yeah," he said, taking another couple of sips. "He was kind of weird in a philosophical way. He didn't seem to belong there, almost as though he was trying to act homeless."

"Act homeless?"

"Yeah, like a rich guy pretending to be poor, you know. Like it didn't really matter because he could always go back to being what he was before."

"Do you think he might have something to do with all this?" Angel asked Larson.

"It sounds like a place to start," he replied.

"We should still have the tape in the library," she said. "It shouldn't take long to find it."

FIVE

THE LAST OF THE ORDER

The dreadlock boy had led them through the harbour streets of Hanoi k'Baja, through a number of narrow passageways, until he finally stopped in an alley littered with rubbish and debris. Pointing to a small doorway roughly boarded over, he told them that was where the last of the Order lay.

"Are you sure?" Jessie asked him.

"Of course I'm sure," the boy told her. "I watched him crawl in there myself."

"You heartless bastard," Luke said. "Why didn't you help him?"

"Why should I? Who ever helped me?"

Luke shook his head in disgust.

"Then you should know more than anyone what it's like to need help."

"Don't lecture me," he retorted. "The street

157

has its own rules, and the first is to look out for yourself."

"I know," Luke said, mellowing a little. "But sometimes you need to look out for others so that they can look out for you."

"Are we going in, or what?" Jessie asked impatiently, going down on her haunches and peering into the darkness where a couple of the boards had been pulled away.

"Don't look at me," the dreadlock boy said. "I've got things to do." And glancing at Luke, added, "People to look out for."

Luke knelt beside Jessie as the boy disappeared. She looked round at him and then pushed herself through into the blackness, Luke following close behind. It was much darker inside than they had thought, and it seemed like a void after the brightness of the morning outside.

Jessie checked her jacket for her cigarette lighter, and found its familiar shape where she had left it, glad that the boy had not taken it. As she sparked its small yellow flame, there came a shuffle ahead of them amongst the debris strewn across the floor, and slowly they stepped towards it.

"Is anyone there?" Luke asked cautiously.

"I hope it's not another cat," Jessie muttered under her breath.

There was no reply, but the shuffling came again.

"We're not here to hurt you," she said into the darkness. "We know what happened to the rest of the Order, and we just want to help."

"How can you help?" came a weak voice just ahead of them.

Jessie held the lighter in the direction of the voice, her eyes straining against the flickering shadows for a figure amongst the boxes and scraps of broken furniture.

"We just want to talk," she said.

"Talk?" the voice said. "What can words heal?"

The weak reach of the flame suddenly caught the edge of a figure lying huddled in the corner of the room amongst the rubble and other debris. Stepping closer, she held out the lighter until it found his face, his expression bloodied and contorted with pain. Bare-chested, he had wrapped his shirt around his leg, its knots dark and glistening, and he made no move to escape, his injuries whilst lying still obviously causing him enough discomfort.

"My name is Mai Turk," he murmured, as

they knelt beside him. "But you are not Depurates."

"No, we're not," Jessie told him.

"But you know what happened to the rest of the Order?"

"We went there because we were told they could help us."

"By who?"

"A man who used to be a disciple of the high priest, Hassan."

"I've heard of this man," Mai told them. "It was said that he followed the spirit of the orkha, but I don't -"

"It's true," Luke said.

"You mean he actually made it to the city of the dead?"

"No," Jessie said to him. "To a world of the living. A place called England. Our home."

Mai tried to sit up, but his face creased with pain and he slumped back down into the rubble. Jessie reached to help him, but he waved her away.

"We followed an orkha the same way as Hassan twenty years ago and found ourselves here," Jessie continued. "You're our only hope of returning. You must help us."

"I've always been taught that the orkhas

guide the souls of the dead to Natura for judgement, I don't know if I could help you even if I wasn't this close to it myself."

"I can not tell you if they do or not. All I know is that they can make a bridge between our two worlds."

Mai looked down, his face one of confusion.

"Can you tell us where we can find these orkhas?" Jessie asked him.

"There are but a few remaining. Old, dying."

"But where are they?" she insisted.

"In the Jume," Mai told her. "But I doubt if they can make bridges anymore."

"We don't have many choices," she said. "We have to try."

"But what of Hassan and his two disciples?" Mai asked them both.

"Two disciples?" Luke said.

Mai nodded, the effort making him wince.

"It was told that one followed his masters good work, while the other plotted to destroy it."

"My master's name was North," Luke said.

"The good one," Mai replied.

"And the name of the bad?"

"Surely you should've guessed by now?" came a voice from behind them.

Jessie turned quickly but it was a voice gravely familiar to her and she had named it before she had even made him out in the gloom.

"Kelso," she said.

"Oh, we do seem to keep meeting under such awkward circumstances, don't we?" he said, smiling as he approached. "I'm beginning to grow rather fond of you."

Two men appeared beside him, each holding torches that they now turned on to illuminate the room. Jessie let the flame go from her lighter and stood to face him. His suit had gone, exchanged for the simple black robes wrapped around him like his accomplices, but there was still gold around his neck and on his fingers, and his expression was still as slick as his words.

"You slaughtered every one of the Order?" she asked him.

"Not every one," he said, glancing at the man crippled on the floor behind her.

"I didn't think even you were capable of that."

"If I thought you could understand, believe

me, I would tell you why."

"Try me," she said.

"The Order seeks to protect a species that cages the souls of the dead," he started. "The human spirit should be allowed to wander free throughout the universe. The orkhas had to die, and the Order along with them."

"You make it sound so honourable."

"I thought I would end up in Natura, the same as Hassan and North -"

"Then why did you go? Why volunteer to be caged?"

"Curiosity," he said simply. "I was still Hassan's disciple, it's just that I didn't agree with all that he taught. When I found another world of the living, I had to find out more."

"So you started Explorer, to look for evidence of orkhas on Earth."

"Now you know why I raged when I found out about the bone you and that shit Larson had kept from me. I'm sorry, Jess, but I just couldn't trust you with something that important."

"But I researched it further than the scientists at Genepool," she said to him.

"You found power, didn't you," he said, smiling. "I knew you would eventually. But I needed Genepool to clone them. I didn't care what happened afterwards."

Jessie hung her head and sighed in frustration.

"Emanuel was an idiot," Kelso continued. "I just needed him to give me what I didn't have. I'm sorry, Jess," he said again.

"That doesn't explain what you're doing here," she said, looking up at him again.

"I came to kill the last of the Order, but now I see there's no point."

"You heartless bastard," she said.

"It's for the good of every human soul," Kelso said, defiantly.   "Including yours and mine. I want to roam the universe when I die, so should you."

Jessie went to speak but there suddenly came a tumultuous splintering of wood as the remaining boards at the door were torn away from its frame, the bright sunlight spilling into the room sending showers of dust swirling in its beams. Standing in front of the open door now were four figures; two large, two small.

The smallest two Jessie and Luke recognised.

One was the dreadlock boy.

The other was Cat Cattah.

"Didn't you believe me," Cat said to Jessie, as he stepped into the debris-littered room towards them, "when I told you I know everyone in this city. I told you I'd find you."

"We trusted you," Jessie said to the boy waiting at the door, but he kept his silence.

"There is no place for naivety in business," Cat continued. "Only money and favours. Am I not right, Mr Kelso?"

"You two know each other?" Jessie asked, incredulous.

"Only by reputation," Cat said, smirking.

"Not all business is the same," Kelso remarked stone-faced. "And standards have their time and their place."

"Don't tell me you give a fuck about morals, Mr Kelso. I've heard the stories."

Kelso bit his lip and said nothing. He knew there were no points to be won and so he didn't press it any further. Cat Cattah smirked again and turned his attention back to Jessie.

"You've cost me a lot," he said to her. "Both revenue and reputation. The man you... killed," he grimaced as he said the word, "was a merchant, an influential man. I had to cover a lot of tracks -"

"That sack of shit deserved to die," Jessie

spat. "It was a shame I couldn't have killed you all."

"He was a customer -"

"He was an animal."

"We are all animals," Cat said to her. "We all have needs. It's just that he was paying to exercise one of his."

"It doesn't matter what words you stick around it, you're still using orphan girls as slaves, as whores, for fucks like you to rape -"

"If you'll excuse me," Kelso said to them all, "I have my own business to attend to. I'll leave you to yours."

"Don't you even care?" Jessie yelled at him, as he started away with his two accomplices. "I thought I knew how low you were, but now I see you're just as bad as them."

Kelso faltered at the remark, pausing mid-stride, but then continued past Cat Cattah and the dreadlock boy towards the doorway without another word, before disappearing out into the alley.

"Which leaves just us again," Cat said.

He nodded to the two hulking men he had brought with him, who began to move towards the pair. Luke reached into his jacket for his gun, but the pocket was empty. He glanced at the boy still standing by the door, who looked away shamefully. They started to back away from the approaching brutes, but they were already in a corner. Stumbling on rubble, Jessie fell to the floor, her hands finding debris all around her. Glancing down, she took hold of a length of wood, and as one of the men reached to grab her, she swung at him.

The length of wood was longer than she had thought and much of it was held beneath the rubble. It moved in the air clumsily as she tried to swing it and the thug easily avoided it, slapping her hard with his huge hand sending her reeling into the dirt.

She looked up to see Luke struggling helplessly with the other, his body being crushed inside a brutish hold. She felt a hand at her back, hauling her up onto her feet before being dragged back towards the door, and caught a flash of Cat's smile before she was taken outside into the bright alley, the sunlight stinging her eyes. Forced onto her knees, she watched as Luke was thrown to the ground beside her. Cat marched grinning towards her.

"There are so many things I've planned to do to you," he said, bringing the back of his hand sharply across her face. Jessie cried out in pain, but he grabbed her head and brought it back to look at him again.

"That was only the first," he said bitterly,

raising his hand again.

Jessie closed her eyes as she waited for the blow, and jumped as instead a gun shot rang out. As she opened her eyes, she saw Cat Cattah teetering in front of her, his jaw dropped, a bullet hole in the centre of his forehead. A line of blood trailed down across his nose like a starved stream, and then he toppled backwards like a slaughtered tree. The air in the alley had suddenly turned silent and still, nobody daring to breathe as they watched the body fall.

Jessie turned to the end of the alley. There stood three men, each dressed in black. In the middle stood Kelso, a gun in his hand, and he wore no expression as they looked at each other. She tried to push herself to her feet, but her legs had no strength in them.

As she crawled to Luke's side, she noticed that his face had blood on it. It was as he opened his eyes to look up at her that she noticed that Cat Cattah's thugs had taken to their heels, perhaps in fear that they might be killed also or perhaps because they too had been prisoners like Ula Mia'h, and they were now freed from their master's hold.

Jessie glanced back at the end of the alley but Kelso had gone, leaving the two of them alone. She waited a few moments before trying to find her feet again, and when she did, dragged Luke back through the door into the building away from the glare of the sun overhead.

"Back again?" Mai called out from the corner of the room.

"Not through choice," Jessie called back. "Now I've got two people who need a doctor."

"I'll be okay," Luke mumbled.

"You'd better watch your step," Mai told her. "You'll be wanted by people higher than Cat Cattah now that you've killed him."

"Hey, it wasn't me who pulled the trigger."

"Do you think anyone's going to care? You'd best get out of the city as quickly as you can."

"As soon as we get you a doctor," she said, "that's exactly what we're going to do."

SIX

TO LEAVE THE CITY

They had left Mai Turk in the hands of a healer he had directed them to. Luke continued to say that he didn't need any medical attention, and that he'd had far worse in Hartwell, adding that they should be trying to find a means of transport to get them to the Jume. Fearful of what Mai had told them about the murder of Cat Cattah, they did their best to hide their faces amongst the crowded streets of Hanoi k'Baja. Buying their breakfast of barbecued fish from a vendor in one of the bustling markets, Luke started up a conversation with him, asking him if he knew where they could hire a guide to take them out of the city.

"Emir Baa," he told them, his booming voice seeming to echo throughout the entire market. "He will take you anywhere for cash."

"And transport," Luke asked him quietly. "Does he have transport?"

"Emir has everything that will take money from your pocket," he laughed.

Following his directions back through the new city to one of the old tenements on the outskirts, they recognised their guide's house from the description the vendor had given them, and it was indeed in as bad repair as he had said. The front door hung awkwardly at what could only be described, and had been, as a hole in the wall. The rough plaster hung from the walls like the skin of a leper's grey complexion and littered the ground outside in small grey drifts, even the patches in need of urgent repair. And the windows sat cracked and shutterless, as blind and lifeless as eyeless sockets.

"It looks abandoned," Luke murmured.

"I'm not surprised," Jessie replied. "If I lived here, I'd abandon it too."

Slowly she approached the door, unsure even as she did so if it would support the assault of knocking. Instead she called out through one of its many fissures, but her voice echoed about inside and there came no reply. Gently she

171

pushed on the door and stepped over the threshold.

"Where are you going?" Luke wanted to know.

"Inside," she replied over her shoulder.

Luke did not want to follow, especially after the slaughter they had stumbled upon the last time they had entered a building unannounced. But as it turned out, there were no dismembered or bloody corpses, just a crudely or even embarrassingly decorated house. The ground floor was sparsely furnished with little or no imagination - a handful of simple chairs, a number of books on a shelf in the living room - and after confirming that nobody was there, they proceeded to climb the uneven staircase to the next floor. Stepping across the wooden landing, Luke following cautiously behind her, Jessie put her head into a couple of rooms only to find them in a similar state to those downstairs; a single mattress, one or two chairs, and a handful of half-full boxes. Inside one of the other rooms she found a long tin bath, a mop of dark hair at one end, a pair of feet sticking out at the other. The boards creaked beneath her feet as she approached, and half expecting to find a drowned body inside, she suddenly leapt back in panic as it rose up in front of her before tumbling out of the bath and onto the floor.

The man clutched at his exposed parts as he scrambled to find his clothes scattered around on the floor. Still panting from shock, and now holding a shirt to his lap, he looked up at them both, his tongue searching fitfully for words.

Still dressing as he hurried downstairs, Emir Baa told them again that he would give them everything that they needed. Jessie thanked him, and stressed that they were probably coming at a bad time because they needed his help straight away.

"Business is bad," he told her. "You come at the best time."

SEVEN

THOSE THAT ARE LEFT BEHIND

Beneath the cold grey sky of Hartwell, Temple stood and watched North sit and stare into the fire. He had grown to respect this man more than any other, and it hurt to see him in such despair. When he had lost everything and found himself wandering alone and lost through the streets, it had been North who had found him; he had given him what little food he had himself, and had shared whatever shelter they could find. Since that time he had shared his fire in winter, his knowledge beneath the blue skies of summer, and his unending wisdom all year round. But over the last few months he had seemed distant, telling him precious little of his thoughts. He had spoken of a woman who had come to see him, and that he had sent the boy to look after her, but much more than that he hadn't said. The last few days had been the worst by far; he had simply sat in front of the fire, staring into its incessant flames, like he did now. And Temple knew not what he should do.

He asked him if he wanted anything to eat once again, but North still did not hear him. He just sat and stared, thoughts hidden and trapped inside his head. Temple turned away, unable to bear to see him in such a state, and started out across the waste ground towards the river. He had taken maybe a dozen steps when he couldn't resist the urge to glance back over his shoulder, but the man at the fire still had not moved.

He thought about the boy as he walked, and realised how much he actually missed him and his energy, although he never would have admitted such. He had only been gone a few days but it seemed like time had slowed to a crawl, the hours dragging themselves long and misshapen like reflections in a circus mirror. Of course he had reprimanded the boy on countless occasions, standards had to be kept up after all, but with his absence coupled with North's despair he was now beginning to grow weary himself.

Stepping out through the abandoned warehouse, he came upon the road that ran from Hartwell through to Morley on the other side of the river. Rarely did he come this way; he needed no reminders of destinations or people with deadlines. But as he wandered across the waste ground, the long grass wrapping itself around his knees, he noticed a dark van crawling at the roadside. He knew vehicles didn't stop on this stretch of road - there was nothing to stop for - yet he watched bemused as the driver seemed uncertain about stopping, concerned perhaps that if he were to stop he might never leave.

For a few moments Temple stood and watched the antics of the van, crawling then stopping, pulling away then stopping again. But as the van rolled closer to him, one of the windows rolled down and a face appeared, calling out to him. At first he thought to ignore it, or even to carry on walking, but he became intrigued as the face called to him again and so he stepped towards the railings by the roadside with interest.

"There was a guy who used to live round here," the face in the van said to him when he was close enough that he didn't have to shout.

"His name is North. You know of him?"

Temple eyed him suspiciously, not knowing whether this was some part of North's despondency or not, and wondered what lay hidden inside the van, and simply told him:

"There are many people who live here."

"We just want to ask him a few questions, that's all."

"We?" said Temple, raising an eyebrow. "What are you? Police?"

The driver at the window laughed, and a woman leaned across from the passenger side to continue, saying:

"We just need to know if he's still around."

"He's around," said Temple. "But would he want to see you?"

"Would a bottle of whiskey help your attitude?" the driver said impatiently.

"You watch your tongue," Temple returned angrily. "I'm no drunk." He turned to the woman. "I'll tell him you're looking for him. Come back tomorrow. If he wants to see you, he'll be waiting."

The panel door of the van slid open and a second man got out and hurried across the pavement towards him.

"There's no time," he said to him urgently.

"A friend of mine has been missing for days. I think this man North may know where she is."

"I understand your concern," Temple relented, as he let out a sigh. "I can take you to him; but only you, no one else."

The man turned and hurried back to the van window. Temple watched as the woman became agitated and he caught only a few of her words. Clearly she did not seem happy with the situation, but he knew he couldn't take so many strangers to see North. He only prayed that this one man he was taking might perhaps lift him a little from his despondency, if he indeed knew what was going on inside his head.

The man hurried back from the van alone, climbing over the rusted metal railings before following Temple back across the wasteground towards the abandoned warehouse. Temple glanced over his shoulder as they stepped into the gutted building; glad to see the van had gone from the roadside and that they were not being followed.

They found North still sitting by the fire, hunched over and staring into the dying embers. Not once did he look up as they approached, nor even when Temple began to stir the embers back to life. The man sat beside North and shared the view of the fire.

"My name is Robert Larson. I want to know if you can help me find my friend, Jessica McHard." When there was no reply, he glanced up at Temple. "Can he hear me?"

"I can hear you," North said, his head still bowed.

"She disappeared a few days ago -"

"We disregard the value of friendship, don't you think?" North murmured, looking up suddenly. "They take so long to make, yet they take only a moment to lose. Careless," he said, looking back into the fire. "We must both be very careless."

"Lost for the moment," Temple said to him, as he laid a few pieces of broken timber onto the hungry embers.

"Lost for good," snapped North.

"I don't know who you have lost," Larson said to him, "and I am sorry, but Jessica spoke of you before she disappeared -"

"And you think I might have something to do with it?"

"No," Larson said. "But I think you might know where she has gone."

"Oh, I know where she has gone," North

told him, looking up again, his eyes as clouded as the blue smoke rising from the fire. "I know where they have both gone."

Larson leant closer to him, desperate to know more.

"They've gone home."

EIGHT

THE RIVER

Emir Baa had taken them down to the harbour, to a small boat tied up at one of the quays. Part of their deal with him had been the Toucouhai that would take them across land from the port of Goa a days journey upstream to the foothills of the Jume. The Toucouhai, or *hai* as they were locally known, were a light brown almost sallow mule-like creature, but with a shaggy coat and small round ears. Sedate and chewing on the feed Emir had given them, they made no fuss of their entry onto the boat and lay down contentedly at the bow. Their guide told them that it was probably a further days journey overland once they left Goa, and when he had at last secured the last of their provisions untied the boat and pushed the craft out into open water.

The sail was smooth for the first few hours, the light wind carrying them gently upstream. Jessie looked up after a while to see Luke heaved over the side of the vessel and went to him.

"Not one for the water?" she asked him.

He glanced up at her, his face fine.

"Fish," he told her, gazing down beneath the boat again. "I've never seen anything like them."

Jessie knelt beside him, holding her hair back with one hand as she leant over to keep it from her face. The river was literally teeming with what seemed like countless species of fish so vast and so varying that it was difficult to spot two alike. Mesmerised she gazed down at them; some she recognised, most she did not. Some took her breath away with their beauty - strings of tiny golden fish threaded like beads that glimmered as they neared the surface - others with flanks of dazzling colours in patterns so strange that when they crossed paths they themselves formed new and wonderful shapes. Others still lurked in the very depths, their presence only known because of their larger darker forms that prowled ominously, following in the shadow of the boat. She turned to Emir who was sat at the back of the boat, his feet up on the arm of the rudder, and asked him:

"What kind of fish are these?"

"All sorts," he replied, shielding the hazy sun from his eyes with his hand. "This river is full of them. Mau, tobaut, scellany - you name it, they're in here."

"What about the big ones?" she wanted to know.

"Big ones?"

"Yes," she said. "The big dark ones swimming down below the others."

"Curkas. But they won't hurt you." But then grinning, added: "Unless you fall overboard."

Jessie sat back away from the water, away from the mau and the tobaut and the curkas, and looked out towards the Jume. They stretched across the horizon like a black jagged line between the sky and the land as though somebody had torn one from the other in a fit of rage. Emir had told them that it was likely to take them at least two days to reach the edge of the mountains, and at their present slow speed she began to doubt the accuracy of this, but it was as she was thinking this that the wind began to pick up behind them. The sails billowed loudly as a band of cloud rolled across the sky to hide the sun. Emir got up from his seat as the wind blustered and he wandered amongst the provisions, checking knots and seeing to the toucouhai.

"Is everything all right?" Jessie asked him, getting to her feet, the boat growing more unsteady by the second.

"I don't like the look of the sky," he told her. "Storms can blow off the ocean whenever they feel like it."

"But we'll be okay?" she said, gripping the mast as the boat lurched to one side.

The guide glanced up at her and then continued to calm the hai who were now beginning to fidget nervously.

"We'll just have to ride it out," he said.

"Can't we tie up at the bank until it blows over," Luke asked, joining Jessie at the mast.

"We're liable to get smashed on the rocks," Emir replied. "We're probably better off in mid-channel."

The wind had whipped up afresh, ravaging the surface of the water, the miraculous fish now gone. Jessie and Luke huddled at the bow, desperately trying to help Emir keep the hai calm and lying down. Rain started to drop from the darkening sky, the wind picking it up and driving it at them in its gusts. The boat was lurching from side to side now, the river raking up waves that lapped over the edges of the boat, filling it with water.

"What are we going to do?" Jessie cried out, but Emir's face answered her plea. The decision was no longer theirs.

The small craft became buffeted by the waves as the wind grew ever stronger, rocking it uncontrollably. One of the boxes slipped its bonds and tumbled across the narrow deck, cracking open and spilling its cargo of bread and preserved meat into the salt water. One of the ropes holding the sail worked itself loose and began to flutter. Emir was after it, stretching as he held on to the edge of the boat. The wind rose up suddenly and took his balance from him. His feet slipped on the wet boards, and snatching at air tumbled into the swirling waters. Jessie and Luke hurried to the side, leaning over waiting for him to surface. His head bobbed from the water some twenty yards away, and below him dark shadows started to play. Emir thrashed at the water to reach the hands outstretched to him, but the storm carried him still further away. Jessie and Luke watched helpless in horror as the dark shapes swirled beneath and around him. Struggling to keep his head above water, he disappeared briefly then surfaced a further ten yards on. The dark shapes had circled him completely now. He went down again, but this time did not surface.

They stared at the spot where he had disappeared and waited but he didn't return.

The wind continued to howl and behind them they heard the hai distressed and panicking. Turning they saw one of them had gotten to its feet, staggering as it fought to find its balance. It let out a bleat of fear as it followed its master, tumbling over the edge and into the open arms of the river. Swallowed whole with barely a ripple, they got to the edge as its silhouette vanished beneath them in the dark water. The remaining two hai were also struggling to their feet now, and both Jessie and Luke put their weight to them to keep them lying down. But panic had overcome them, and as the boat rocked right over onto its side, the river rushed in, capsizing the small vessel in a heart beat.

Jessie surfaced amongst the cargo of boxes

bobbing around her head. Thrashing to keep afloat she looked round frantically for Luke, and there, some twenty yards from her she could see him floating face down. As she started to swim desperately towards him, she noticed the dark shapes of the curkas swirling beneath her, but she struggled on, the distance between her and Luke halved now. As she reached him, she pulled back his head. His eyes closed and lips parted, she instinctively put her mouth to his and tried to blow air into it. Still unconscious, she took hold of him and started towards the bank, grateful that the tide was carrying her towards it.

With the dark curkas prowling just beneath her, she waited for them to snatch at their feet or drag them beneath the surface, but as she came to the first of the rocks at the bank, she almost raced up out of the water, pulling every last effort of strength out of her limbs to haul both herself and Luke away from the curkas reach.

Standing with her chest heaving on the slick grassy bank, she stared back across the turbulent surface of the river. The boat had gone, and only a handful of boxes bobbing amongst the waves marked their efforts. Emir

Baa and the three hai were nowhere to be seen, all drowned or being rapaciously devoured somewhere beneath the surface. She looked away in horror and turned back to Luke. He was still unconscious, and after pushing herself to her feet started to drag him further up the bank and past the treeline, where she managed to find some partial shelter away from the sting of the wind and the rain.

Collapsing from fatigue beside him and holding his head in her arms, she closed her own eyes and waited for the storm to pass.

NINE

SECRETS WHISPERED THAT
BIND TWO HEARTS

When she awoke she noticed that Luke was no longer beside her. Concerned, she sat up and found him down by the edge of the river, heaved over the rocks. Getting to her feet she stepped down the bank towards him. He looked up at her as she knelt beside him, his face flushed and flecked with spittle. She put her hand to his tousled hair, and whispered:

"Not one for the water."

"Something hit me when the boat went over," he replied, feeling the back of his head. "I think my lungs are full of water."

He coughed up another mouthful.

"I think we should move away from the river," Jessie suggested, studying the still-overcast sky. "If we head through the trees, we might come across a village or something."

Luke looked around them. The river was lined with trees and rocks in all directions. They couldn't even see the city of Hanoi k'Baja any longer.

"I don't think we have any choice," Jessie added.

Luke reluctantly got to his feet, and still a little unsteady, walked back up to the treeline with Jessie.

The pines were tall and dense, their canopy shielding much of the sky as they walked, making the day seem darker than it was. They also became aware of a strange birdcall high above them, a weird chatter that echoed inanely through the branches, the creature making such a call profoundly elusive until at last they noticed one.

Perfectly camouflaged in the boughs of the pines, their feathers replaced by dense green spines, they looked down with calls of curiosity, the gift of flight surely impossible. They caught sight of such absurd creatures as they strayed too close to a small flock foraging on the ground and they rose startled high into the air, bristling like a plague of emerald porcupines.

Soon they noticed a clearing up ahead, and

as they broke out of the trees, they realised just
how dark the sky had become. They could see
the black ragged line of the Jume now the
horizon   was   visible,   but   the   sun   had
disappeared behind it and the plains were
almost as dark as the starless heavens above
them.

"We should stop here until morning," Jessie
said to him, searching her jacket for her
cigarettes.

"I think I can see a road," Luke told her,
squinting out into the gloom.

She pulled out the damp packet, cursing it
before looking up to follow his gaze.

"I don't see -"

"There," he said, pointing.

"It's a long way off yet," she told him. "It'll
be too dark to see anything by the time we get
there."

"At least there's firewood here," he agreed,
and started back into the pines.

"So why were you following Kelso?" Luke
asked her later, as he held the flame from her
cigarette lighter beneath a heap of brushwood.

Jessie looked up at him blankly.

"You followed him to the Genepool building. Why?"

"He was up to something. I didn't know what at the time."

Luke watched her as she stared at the hungry flames licking eagerly over the dead kindling.

"You're not going to tell me, are you?"

"Tell you what, Luke?"

"Anything."

Jessie looked up at him again. His face was pained and she realised then just how much she had been keeping things from him. She'd been so caught up in her own thoughts that she hadn't noticed how much he had wanted to be close to her.

"We've been through so much, Jess," he said to her. "I deserve to know something about what's going on."

"You're right," she said, sighing. "But it's a depressing story."

"Tell me anyway."

Jessie looked at him for a moment and then took a seat on the ground, wondering as she did so whether she should indeed tell him her story or not. But she started readily enough, and before she knew it, she was soon pouring out details that she hadn't thought about in a very long time.

"I knew what Kelso was like even before I started working for him. My uncle, Clay Munroe, was his partner years ago, and they made quite a name for themselves - well, one of them did anyway. My uncle stayed out in the field while Kelso handled the business side, taking all the credit."

"He said he made all the discoveries?"

"And more besides. Kelso sent him out to the remotest of places, cutting him off from civilisation most of the time, and feeding him a string of mediocre supplies and bullshit. When he eventually found out, Kelso cut him. But by that time he had enough money, contacts and new scientists to continue the company."

"And you went to work for him knowing all this?"

"I know, I was stupid," she said, shaking her head. "I thought I could get something back for my uncle - cheat the devil - something like that."

"But he got you before you could get him."

"He sure did," she closed her eyes as she pushed her hands through her hair. "And you now what really pisses me off?" she said to him, looking up. "I didn't learn my lesson, and he fucked me over again."

Luke was silent beside her. He didn't know whether to laugh at such absurdity or cry with her. Instead he just stared at her with indecision.

"I know what you're thinking," she said to him. "You're thinking loser, right?"

"Not at all," he said plainly. "Sometimes we learn from our mistakes. But sometimes we want something so badly we're willing to take that risk again. It hurts, sure, but it can hurt more regretting taking that risk again."

"When did you get so wise?" she asked him, smiling.

He looked down into the fire, its flames the only light now in the blackness around them, but Jessie reached out with her hand to lift his chin. Leaning forward, she put her lips to his, kissing him gently, his eyes open and questioning.

As their lips parted he went to speak but she silenced him with a second kiss, her arms drawing him towards her into an embrace. Her fingers sought to undo his shirt, to touch the skin of his chest, but he raised his own to stop her. She let him have his way and dropped her hands to his lap. His arms fell and lay dormant at his sides even as she began to unbuckle his jeans, his tongue at last enticed from his mouth as she parted his lips with her own.

Jessie managed to pull his jeans down over his thighs despite his lethargy but it was too dark to see the luxury of his bare flesh, and she closed her eyes to dream it all as she took hold of his rigid member and began slowly to slide her hand up and down its length, Luke exhaling heavily through their kiss. Jessie left him reluctantly to pull her own jeans down, his arms rising to accept her embrace this time as she sat astride him, allowing him to enter her as she eased herself down over him. He shuddered as she put her mouth hard to his and began to rock gently over him, squeezing him hard inside her. She hadn't realised how long it had been since she had been with a man and the tremors now burning inside her were urging her onward like she had never known.

Soon she was pushing as hard as she could, working herself down on top of him, her eyes clenched now as she threw back her head. A handful of breaths came heavy in front of her, and as she felt Luke's hips shudder, she herself came, stammering a sob as she grabbed hold of the hair at the back of his head.

Kissing him with her eyes still lidded, she rolled with him onto his back, and there she lay panting with her head in the arch of his neck.

"I... I love you," Luke murmured quietly. Then he added, "I've never said that before."

"You'll get used to it," Jessie replied warmly, kissing his neck.

Luke arched his back a little and Jessie felt his cock begin to slide from her.

"Leave it where it is," she said to him. "I want to feel it some more."

She felt his hand go to her head, his fingers gently raking at her hair. Her senses began to swim with delirium, and feeling the heat from his body and the heave of his chest, slowly began to drift from consciousness. She felt the chill of the night breeze cold on the sweat of her skin, and she held Luke more tightly, until all her pleasures became one promised sleep.

But it was not a dreamless sleep.

She found herself riding blind through a midnight forest, as dark and as fathomless as the black sky looming through the canopy above her. It was not until she broke through into a clearing and came to a halt beside a cabin that she realised that she was not alone. Two men dismounted beside her, both dressed from head to foot in black robes and both of them carrying weapons. She didn't know what it was that they intended to hunt, and she watched unable to ask as they approached the cabin.

She looked around her as they disappeared

inside. A stream babbled lazily just ahead of her, she could see it now there were stars to light the ground. Beyond that rose the purple-black face of the Jume, looming ominously like a thunderhead against the night sky. She looked back as the two hunters emerged from the cabin, their arms laden with food and supplies, but they were back riding hard again towards the mountains before she could ask after the cabin-dwellers hospitality.

The foothills were steep yet her mount was equal to its demands, finding the surest rocks and threading a path higher and higher until they reached a narrow passage that would take them down into the valley beyond. Jessie glanced round briefly as the two other riders started down. Below her she could see the cabin by the stream, and the forest she had ridden through; beyond that stretched open plains and a road that twisted back round to the city of Hanoi k'Baja in the far distance. Then turning her back on it, she urged her steed forward down into the valley and became enveloped by the might of the Jume.

TEN

THE TRUTH ABOUT THE ORPHAN

The black cab turned the corner into Cromwell Road, its tyres skidding on the slick tarmac. The rain had kept away all morning, saving itself for the deluge that had erupted some twenty minutes ago, making the hunt for elusive streets close to impossible.

"I tell you there ain't no Gallows Lane up this road," the cabbie said again over his shoulder.

"And I'm telling you there is," North retorted. "It's just a little way -"

"I've been driving these streets since I was nineteen and I never -"

"There!" North yelled, grabbing the cabbie's shoulder with one hand and pointing out through the misted windscreen with the other.

He yelped with surprise, stamping hard on

the brakes. The wheels locked instantly on the wet road, tossing both North and Larson forward off their seats in the back.

"Jesus, mister..." the cabbie stammered, clutching at his chest.

"This is it?" Larson asked, staring out through the condensation at the narrowest of alleyways.

"Can you wait for us?" North asked as he opened the door. "Five minutes."

"Sure, why not?" the cabbie replied. "It'll give me time to add this place to my map."

Larson followed North across the sidewalk and into the alley. There was partial shelter from the rain behind its walls but the wind that came at their faces carried it in its gusts.

"Tell me again who this guy is?" Larson asked, hurrying beside him.

"Hassan was the high priest of an order created to worship, and ultimately protect, a species known as orkhas. It was believed that these orkhas carried the souls of the dead to Natura, a great city where they were judged. But there was a second group who sought to destroy these creatures, convinced that without them their souls would be free to roam the universe. Hassan told both his disciples one day that -"

"Both?" Larson said. "I thought there was just you."

"No, no, my friend. There were two of us."

North stopped for a moment to glance up and down the length of the alley. Then he began to walk again.

"He never told us why he wanted to go to Natura," he continued. "Only that he had to see the city for himself. The day we left to go into the heart of the Jume to find the orkhas, was the day of the fire."

Larson looked at him blankly.

"Our temple burned to the ground that day. We saw the smoke behind us as we travelled, but -"

They came to a sudden halt as they reached a dead end. North turned round and looked back the way they had come and frowned. Larson followed him as he started back, retracing their steps, the wind now blowing the rain at their backs. He studied this man as they walked, so unlikely a vagrant he thought he could've found. So absurd were his stories of other worlds that he would not have believed them except that they now seemed so plausible. Perhaps it was because he had now found a direction to ease his frustration, or perhaps because there was something wonderful to be found, something that Jessie had already stumbled upon. But whatever it was, he suddenly became aware that he felt no anxiety or trepidation about being alone with a leader of street people, trying to find an unknown holy man in an unknown alley. And it seemed strangely fitting that this was the only route to discovering where Jessie had gone.

"A door," North murmured, pointing to a section of the wall ahead of them.

"I don't see how we could have missed it before."

North stepped forward and knocked against the wooden frame. They stood, straining to hear any movement from the other side, but there was silence. North knocked again, and this time they could hear the faint shuffling of feet, and pressing his ear to the damp wood, he could make out the wheezing breath of somebody waiting on the other side.

"Hassan? This is North. We need to talk."

He glanced round at Larson standing beside him whose expression seemed dubious.

"Hassan?" he tried again. "I know you're there, I can hear your breathing. Get rid of that pipe - it's fucking your lungs up."

There was silence for a moment, and then there came the rattle and slide of bolts being drawn from the other side. The door opened a little and there before them stood a short old man gazing up at them. Larson watched uneasily as the two men stared at each other without exchanging a word, and not once did the old man acknowledge him.

"I expect there's some reason for you being here," the old man said at last.

"It's the boy," North stated. "He's gone home."

Hassan stared hard at him, his eyes widening so slightly it was hardly noticeable in the gloom, but apart from that he seemed unfazed. Then he said:

"You'd best come in."

Larson still had not been introduced, or even acknowledged, but he followed both teacher and student down a flight of steps into a small room below. A fire was burning inside, casting flickering shadows up onto the walls. Hassan took his seat at the hearth, leaving his two visitors to find their own, before taking up his pipe from a table beside him. He looked up at his pupil as he started to fill the bowl, paused, and then irritably set it back on the table along

202

with the nugget of tobacco.

"There was an experiment," North started. "They created an orkha from a bone this man found."

"And just how did this man find the bone of an orkha?"

"This man," Larson interjected, drawing the old mans attention for the first time, "found it on another planet."

Hassan stared at him, a question waiting at his lips.

"I don't think it was your world," Larson told him. "This planet was desolate - dead from solar radiation."

"I always believed they could travel to other worlds," the old man murmured. "Didn't I always say that?"

"That you did," North said. "But the problem is, what do we do about Luke?"

"And Jessie," Larson added.

Hassan looked at him.

"The girl who came to see me?" he asked incredulously. "Surely she hasn't gone as well. But -"

"It was Jessie who started all this."

"I sent Luke to watch over her, and he must have followed her through," North said. "But he doesn't know who he really is."

"You're sure of that?"

North nodded.

"What do you mean, who he really is?" Larson wanted to know.

"Luke was an illegitimate child," Hassan began, sighing. "His mother was found in the foothills of the Jume. People from a village nearby found her after the attack -"

"Attack?"

"Yes, but by what nobody was sure. Some thought she had been set upon by wolves because of the gashes and bites across her body, others said a gang travelling through the mountains, but a few suggested the unthinkable, that she'd been savagely raped by at least one orkha. And of course this only heightened the tensions in those eager to destroy the entire breed." He picked up his pipe without looking, pushing his fingers over its familiar curves, then he glanced down at it and put it back cursing. "When the child was born, there was no doubt."

"Child?" Larson gaped.

"The woman smuggled the creature to me. She didn't know what else to do with it. The baby seemed human, but... but its skin... its body and legs were disfigured with the zebra-stripes of the orkha. She left it with me, telling me that she'd return the next day to collect it."

"And you never saw her again?"

"Oh, we saw her again. She was found with a rope around her neck, hanging like a sack of grain."

"So you had to keep the child."

"We kept the child, but I wanted to dash its brains, to save it from a life of cruel persecution. But I couldn't do it. That was when I knew it was time to go to Natura - to satisfy what I believed, and so that they could take the child if they wanted him."

"But instead you ended up here."

"Stranded and lost," Hassan said, shaking his head dismally. "North took the boy to raise him."

"It wasn't much of a life on the streets," North admitted sadly.

"But you couldn't very well take him to social services," Larson conceded. "He'd be ridiculed as a freak, poor kid."

"When he started asking questions about himself, as I knew he would, I didn't know what to tell him. I couldn't bring myself to tell him the truth, I loved him too much for that. He wanted to know about his markings -"

"And now you're afraid he might discover the truth."

"Oh, he'll discover the truth all right," North said. "As soon as he sees an orkha, he'll know who he is."

"But is there a way for us to go after them?" Larson asked Hassan. "After all, that's why we're here."

"If there was," he told him, shaking his head, "do you think I'd be sitting here waiting to die under alien skies?"

Larson looked down, unable to look at him now, and said:

"No, I suppose not."

"Your kind started all this," Hassan said to him. "Why now do you come to me?"

"My kind stumbled through it all trying to fight ignorance. You have knowledge."

"Knowledge, maybe. But knowledge destroys wisdom. And now I know that it was unwise for me to have come here." He paused, and then smiled at his own joke. "There's nothing I can do for you. But if you should see the boy again," he said, turning to North, "tell him that I'm sorry; sorry for allowing him to live in a world that could only ever bring him hopelessness and solitude."

ELEVEN

ECHOES OF MURDER TRAILS

Jessie opened her eyes to the bright clear sky of a beautiful early dawn. Covered with her jacket, its warmth and comfort was a poor substitute for those of the lovers she had been wrapped in the previous night, and sitting up saw him re-kindling the fire, a small pile of sticks beside him. He had his back to her and she watched him for a while. As he started laying the wood on the fire he glanced round at her and saw her staring at him.

"I didn't mean to wake you," he said.

"You didn't."

Luke turned back to tend to the fire, lazily playing a stick into its flames. Jessie got to her feet and began pulling her jeans back on, and noticed Luke glance up at her out of the corner of her eye, his look lingering too long to be casual, curious to see her naked skin by the light of day. He looked back into the fire as she started towards him, busy with the stick once again.

"Are you okay?" she asked him.

Luke said that he was without looking up at her.

Jessie went down on her haunches and lifted his chin like she had the night before, kissing him gently before saying:

"Thank you for last night."

His face radically lightened and she was glad to see him return her smile. He started to murmur something but she put her finger to his lips to silence him. Though she wanted nothing more than to hear his words, they still had a purpose, and like furtive lovers those words would have to wait until the welcoming embrace of nightfall.

Kicking dirt onto the small fire, the two of them started off across the plains toward the road. With an ache in their bellies they hoped the road might lead them to a house or a village where they could eat before they reached the slopes of the Jume. Neither of them could dare to suggest the inevitable if they should arrive at the foothills with no supplies or directions.

Luke had suggested that they take the road to return to the city, but with the cloud of Cat Cattah's murder hanging over them like an executioner's axe they had decided that whatever lay ahead - even if it be starvation or insanity - it would be preferable to whatever punishment the law of Hanoi k'Baja could give them.

It took them the best part of two hours to set foot on the dirt road. They passed little traffic as they travelled, the black wall of the Jume looming ever larger before them, but what few there were seemed to be farmers or prospectors collecting supplies or taking their harvest to the now distant city behind them. One such wagon, its rickety back laden with tools and canvas and coffee, rumbled slowly past them, its driver glancing down with much curiosity at them both. His skin was a subtle shade of green, and he bore a striking plumage of blue and gold feathers from his shoulders and back that ruffled in the wind. Luke called up to him as he nodded in courtesy, asking him where the road was leading them, and if there were any villages along the way.

"I'm headed to Amst, which is the first village you'll come to," the farmer said to them, his voice bright with harmonious accents. He then asked them if they knew anything of the scandal from the city.

"What scandal?" Jessie asked him in return.

"Apparently one of the whores of the northern parts had been lying in wait for the owner of a brothel, and after slitting his throat, had cut off his cock and forced it into his own mouth."

The farmer laughed at this, the bright feathers on his back rustling again as the wind caught them again.

"Does anyone know who did it?" Jessie asked, trying to seem only mildly curious.

"No," he replied. "It's all bullshit anyway. Everyone knows he ran his whorehouse with kids he took off the street. Anyone could have killed him."

"You don't think they'll catch the killer then?"

"Hell, if I'd have met him, I probably would have slit the bastard's throat myself."

Accepting his offer and climbing up into the wagon beside the farmer, they discussed the matter no further as they travelled. The road eventually left the plains and entered a tall forest, the sweet tang of pine lightening the air with its fresh perfume. The familiar calls of the emerald porcupines echoed throughout the treetops, yet Jessie felt a little uneasy as they rocked about over the uneven dirt road. It wasn't until after maybe half an hour's travel, when they passed a track beaten through the undergrowth into the trees, that she realised why.

"I think we should stop," Jessie whispered to Luke, tugging on his sleeve.

"Stop?" he said to her. "What on earth for?"

"I don't know. I think maybe we should try that track."

"Why? You know this road will take us to Amst where we can hopefully get something to eat, and even find someone to take us up into the mountains."

"I know, I know," she said, glancing over her shoulder at the track, its entrance nearly out of sight now. "It's just... I don't know... it seems like the way to go, that's all."

She turned back and saw the concern on his face. She knew he was right, they had to continue to the village if only for the sake of their hunger. Yet she wanted to travel into the forest, to ride swiftly like she had with the two hunters, and maybe thank the cabin-dweller by the stream. But she knew it had only been a dream, and the ache in her stomach made her take Luke's hand.

"Okay," she said to him. "We'll go on to Amst."

TWELVE

CAPRICAAN

The sun was high above them when the road eventually widened and the first of the buildings of the village came into view. There were children playing in the road and amongst the trees, chasing each other with their games, wearing camouflaged headbands of bracken and grass. The villagers, like the children, were as green as the farmer beside them, their shoulders and backs ablaze with feathers a palette of different colours; rich hues of yellows and crimsons and golds. Most looked up at them riding in on the wagon, some even waving their welcome.

"Seems a happy enough place," Luke remarked.

"It's beautiful," Jessie sighed. "I'd be happy if my life was here."

There seemed to be children playing everywhere; in the narrow spaces between the timber houses, on the village green where the farmer now pulled the wagon to a halt, even the branches of the trees seemed to have children hiding and swinging in them, their laughter and songs also rising out of every window along the street. They thanked the farmer as he steered his wagon back out along the road, and they couldn't help smiling at each other at the peace and freedom around them.

Luke suggested that he try and find food for them both, and perhaps some directions, even a guide, while Jessie stayed on the green to rest. She watched him go before she lay back on the soft grass, relaxing beneath the warming sun, the release of the children's voices soothing her like a lullaby.

At first there seemed to be as many games as there were happy faces, but after a while it became apparent to her that they were all part of just one game. The children they had seen in the forest with heads of bracken wore black cloaks which they wrapped around themselves, hiding in the shadows of the trees and houses. And it was they who held the sticks and chased the other children, muddy black stripes daubed across their backs, tainting their richly coloured feathers. She watched as these painted children would run in circles, in feigned panic, until touched with one of the sticks. They would then dance cartwheels of pain and roll to the ground. When all the stripes were still, they would repeat the same game to the same chorus of laughter and song.

It was a welcome sight to see such happiness after the horrors they had witnessed in Hanoi k'Baja, and she closed her eyes to soak up the warmth of the beautiful day. She found it difficult to concentrate on any of the thoughts in her head longer than a few moments and it soon occurred to her that it was because of the children's voices. Like the variety of their games, the once exquisite beauty of their song soon became banal with their monotony. And with her eyes closed it became even more insidious. What had once been a lilting chorus had turned to a sickening din, bringing unease with its dirge, having no crescendo or fall.

Looking up she saw the same game across the village green around her, children daubed with stripes rolling to the ground only to leap up again, despite how much she wanted them to lay as still and as silent as death itself, if only for a moment. Thoughts partially formed in her head about the brutality of wishing children to die, but even these could not grasp the hooks of her brain long enough to take root. As she went to put her hands to her head, she heard her name being called behind her. She turned and fought to focus on the two figures approaching. One of them called her name again, and she was glad of something familiar to concentrate on, and with his face as well as his voice to comfort her, she had almost settled by the time he reached her.

"Are you okay?" Luke asked her, kneeling down beside her. "You were swaying about. I thought you were going to pass out or something."

"I was feeling faint, I think," she said, rubbing at her face with the palms of her hands. "Perhaps its just hunger."

Luke set a long roll of bread, a number of spiced sausages and some fruit down in front of her, which she eagerly took up and started eating.

"I've found someone to take us up into the mountains," Luke said to her as he watched her eat. He ushered forward the small boy he had brought with him. "This is Capricaan."

The boy nodded his welcome as Jessie looked up at him.

"He says he knows where we can find the last of the orkhas."

"The last?" Jessie said.

"There are only a few left alive," Capricaan told her. "They're really old and don't travel much."

"And you can take us to them?"

The boy nodded indifferently, his feathers iridescent as they fanned.

It was then that Jessie noticed that he was the first child she had seen in the village who was not part of the zebra-chasing game. Looking at him now as she tasted one of the fruits Luke had brought, she couldn't help wondering why. His attention was solely with them, and although he seemed as airy and aloof as any child, his hands didn't itch to pick up a stick for beating or his feet to carry him away to chase or to hunt.

Capricaan looked up suddenly and caught her studying him but he seemed neither disturbed nor offended by her scrutiny; she was the curiosity here after all, not he. His indifference and calm seemed strangely pleasing to her and she smiled at him. He returned her smile, and said:

"We can pick up some blankets and food from my parent's house before we go."

Jessie agreed, telling him that they'd probably have to stay up in the mountains for a while.

"For how long?" the boy enquired.

"I don't know," she said. "I'm not even sure what we'll discover up there."

THIRTEEN

FATHER AND SON ACROSS A DIVIDE

Once out of the village, Capricaan led them along a winding stream that skirted the foothills. Some way upstream they came upon three enormous posts driven into the rock, each one elaborately painted with rich colours. As they got closer they discovered their surfaces to be carved and scored with innumerable symbols and pictures. The boy had continued past indifferently and only after he'd taken a dozen more steps did he realise he was alone and turned back for them.

"It's a kind of totem," he told them, anticipating their bewilderment as he sat down on one of the larger boulders. "Both a warning and a memorial."

"Of what?" Luke asked.

"Orkhas are hated around here more than

anywhere. It's to keep them up in the mountains."

"Why are they so hated?" Jessie wanted to know. "Are they dangerous?"

Capricaan paused, and then said:

"My mother told me a story of a woman, one of your kind, who was attacked by an orkha here on this very spot. She was torn to ribbons and her limbs devoured, yet she managed to return home to her cabin upstream. We'll pass it on the way."

"You don't seem afraid of the orkhas," Luke remarked.

"It's only a story," the boy replied, shrugging.

"Sounds more like a legend."

"In time, maybe," Capricaan said to him. "The story's only a couple of decades old."

The boy got up from his seat and started away back upstream, Luke and Jessie following behind. His legend-to-be troubled her somewhat as they walked across the smooth rocks, images of orkhas now as predators playing on her mind as well as her nerves. Juggling such concerns with the knowledge that these creatures were the point of their journey in the first place did not help to calm her. Caught up with visions in her head, she did not notice the cabin until they had stopped beside it.

Built on the edge of the forest overlooking the stream, the cabin seemed as beautiful and as desolate a place to live as she could possibly dream of. Walking round to the front she noticed a partial trail leading out into the trees into the depths of the forest, its path disappearing amongst the undergrowth. Jessie became uneasy as she studied the familiar face of the cabin, the same cabin she had waited outside while the two men swathed in black robes had entered so furtively. The need to know more, and even perhaps to see the face of whoever lived inside, overwhelmed her and she approached the door as if in a waking dream. She became aware of Luke calling her name somewhere behind her but she was already reaching for the door, knocking on the wood. Her mind conjured images of what the two riders had seen inside that she had not, and wondered briefly if her identity was irrelevant only in dreams, but such thoughts were snatched from her as the door suddenly opened and a large grizzled man stood gazing at her, a hunting knife poised in one hand. Jessie stumbled back as he stepped out into the glare of sunlight, demanding to know who she was.

"It's okay," Capricaan piped, as he and Luke appeared at Jessie's side. "She's with me."

"And that's meant to comfort me?" the man mumbled irritably. "Damn fool boy."

Capricaan grinned, enjoying his feral reputation, and went to lead Jessie away.

"The woman who was attacked, she lived here?" Jessie asked.

The man winced with pain and seemed almost to stumble in front of her.

"Yeah, she lived here," he said angrily. "She was my wife. What is it to you?"

Capricaan took her by the arm and tried to urge her away but she resisted his efforts, wanting to continue with the cabin-dweller.

"We saw three totems beside the stream -"

"Poles ain't the answer," he muttered. "I'd take them down myself but for the sakes of the villagers."

"Why take them down?"

"Borla can't kill them if they're warned away," the boy interceded.

"You don't look much like hunters to me," Borla commented, staring the boys travellers up and down. "You ain't trying to make friends with them devils like this insane kid, are you? They need killing. I do what I can, but," he slapped the side of his leg, "I can't get up in the mountains like I used to. So I do what I can for those that come through here. Food, weapons, even money sometimes."

"You pay them?" Jessie said.

"I do anything I can that will destroy every last one of them," he replied gravely.

Jessie looked at him. She could see a warmth beneath his grizzled face and words, but she could not help pressing him further.

"Who were the last to come through?" she asked him.

"Three men, night before last. Only two came in -"

"For food?"

"All I could spare."

"Dressed in black?"

Borla narrowed his eyes as he nodded.

"You know them?" he asked her.

"I don't know," she murmured, shaking her head.

"You're going up into the Jume, aren't you?" he said to them. "Please, leave it alone. What do you expect to find up there?"

"A way back home. A future."

"I loved my wife," Borla told them, as they turned to leave. "She was everything to me. We were trying for a family, for a son, but when she was attacked... I got only part of her back."

"We heard how she was dismembered... we're sorry..."

"She wasn't dismembered, at least not physically. She was torn and covered in blood when I found her, clothes ripped half naked. Her wounds healed but she grew worse over the months that followed; staring, talking to herself, we all expected her to get better. Until one day she starts screaming like she's insane, clutching at her belly - it was all I could do to stop her from slicing herself to shreds or dashing her own brains." Borla was pacing now, wringing his hands and pushing them over his head in despair. "I felt so hopeless, seeing her like that... I felt sometimes like... like ending her sickness myself. I feel sometimes like ending my own..."

"But you didn't though," Jessie said, putting her hand to his arm.

"No, I didn't," he said grimly, shaking his head. "One morning I woke to find her gone. I searched the forest and the mountains for days, expecting to find her with her throat open or her skull cracked and empty. But I found nothing. That was how I broke my leg," he put his hand to his crooked limb again. "I slipped from a ledge onto the rocks below. Each day I wonder if I was lucky to escape with my life."

"So you never found out what happened to your wife?"

"Oh, I found out alright," he told her. "About three months later, I found out she'd hung herself in Hanoi k'Baja. Not only did insanity take her life, it also took that of our son."

"Your son?"

"I knew she was pregnant," he said, heaving a breath. "She tried to keep it from me. She must have thought... must have known... the baby was..." Borla put his hands to his face as he started to heave with sobs. "Such a creature... I would have killed it myself."

Borla turned and stumbled back towards his cabin. Jessie went to go after him, but Capricaan stopped her.

"Best to leave him," he said to her. "So far from the promise of his son, there's nothing we could do."

*   *   *

The dream she'd had beneath the plain's starless sky the night before had intrigued her more than anything else. Vivid while she had slept - riding hard through the trees and mountains with mysterious cloaked hunters to either side of her - she still had little idea of what her purpose had been or would be, or even of who she was. Had it been a map of her future, she wondered, as they followed the boy up through the foothills, pictures glimpsed from a subconscious eager to invent? If so, then it was of little help to her, except in the revelation of hindsight.

As they reached the first of the ridges that would take them down into the valley beyond, she turned to look back and saw now what she had seen through her dream-travellers eyes: the plains beyond the forest reaching out to the distant city, down to her right the village of Amst and its children of the hunt, and below the cabin, Borla's home filled with his own memories and dreams, remembered and redreamt past the point of anguish and agony. Turning away, she followed Capricaan and Luke who had already stepped into the narrow ridge and had dipped below the reach of the sun's light.

Close to the valley floor, it was decided that it was too dark to continue safely. Feeling the warmth from the small scrubwood fire, Jessie wrapped her blanket tightly around her, the chill of the valley wind disorientating her, even in the drifts of sleep.

She could see the black hunters ahead of her entering a cave, a faint light emanating from inside beyond them. She became aware that she was afraid, but of what she couldn't make out. The light, perhaps, or what was making that light. It seemed strange for her to be fearful of such beautiful radiance, its blues almost resonating off the tunnel walls with each step she took, and yet it seemed so familiar to be surrounded by it. Perhaps it was not fear she felt after all, but awe.

One of the shadowed hunters quickened his pace ahead of her, calling something over his shoulder that she couldn't catch. But he had barely taken two more steps when his legs suddenly went from under him - precisely, his legs went away from him. She stood in the tunnel and watched both his limbs cartwheel across the rock in a spatter of blood. His torso dropped awkwardly to the floor, but she was still too far to hear his screams and pleas. She saw something appear almost from the blue light itself, its glistening body bright and incandescent, black zebra stripes dashed around it like razor scars. Within an instant the hunter's chest was open, his scarlet innards rising high into the air like bloodied ropes and balloons, followed moments later by his black scarfed head, which hit the ground and rolled to meet its lost legs.

The creature of light turned briefly, its face a blur of needle teeth and ebony jewel eyes. And then it was gone, dissolving back into the pure blue of its own existence beyond the end of the tunnel.

Jessie woke shivering, her blanket around her knees, gooseflesh raised from the chill of the wind as it whipped across her sweat-soaked clothes. She dragged the blanket back up over her, and only then did she realise that she was trembling, her heart scuttling in her chest like crab claws. She felt Luke stir beside her and edged closer to him, nestling against his body to steal some of his warmth.

Details of the dream were already slipping from her mind's grasp despite how she fought to understand their significance and their vivid potency. She had no idea who the mysterious hunter was, or why he should perish so horrifically, and even as she huddled beside Luke hoped she would never have to get that close to the creature of light. She also hoped that this too was not another premonition which only in hindsight would become clear.

Jessie reached out beneath the blanket and put her arm around Luke. She only wanted his touch, and not that of the creature born of the blue light. She hadn't expected dangers at the start of their journey to find their way home, although even that in hindsight was naive, but knew that only by facing those dangers and the fears that fed them would they see their destiny. And that, she knew, would be worth facing such teeth and ebony jewel eyes for.

FOURTEEN

THEY COULD COME BACK

The drive back through Hartwell was a quiet one. The two men were lost to despair, thoughts so heavy that even the cabbie knew to keep his conversation to himself. Their meeting with Hassan had brought them no revelation, and only left greater concern and hopelessness, their only hope of salvation halted at a dead end. Larson glanced at the man slumped beside him, his face wretched and cast downward at the floor, and said:

"We could go back to the labs, there might be something to find there."

"I don't want to see any of it," North replied solemnly.

Larson told him that he understood, adding that something might happen soon.

"I've waited over half my life telling myself that - waiting for a chance to go home, to see the sky again - and that's all I've done; wait - I've nothing else to do."

"You said something about hoping they would end up near the city where you used to live."

"It's the only place I know," North said, looking up at him. "But they could be anywhere. We don't really know anything about orkhas, only that they can travel to other dominions, maybe even dimensions, as easily as we can travel from room to room."

"Hassan never mentioned -"

"Hassan didn't want to commit himself to such possibilities, I think it fucked with his head. And it can, if you think about it too much."

"So what do you think?" Larson asked him.

North sighed heavily as he stared out of the grimy window at the wet sprawling city they were driving through.

"You know of one world," he said. "I know of two. Who's to say there isn't three, or four, or hundreds, thousands?"

"And orkhas can build the bridges between them all..."

North tried to smile, a glow of energy warming in him that he hadn't felt since his first inspiring days as a disciple of the Bening Tai'Orkha. But it failed just as quickly as it had sparked, certain that he would never set foot on that bridge ever again. He had glimpsed the edge of possibilities and had lost it before the grip had been tightened sufficiently enough to hold on.

"If Luke has orkha blood in him," Larson suggested. "Then could he not have such abilities?"

"It's possible," North said grimly. "But with so many worlds..."

"They could come back."

North looked up at him suddenly, and said: "Would you?"

FIFTEEN

EXTINCTION

The route they were following was taking them higher into the Jume. With the snowline growing ever closer they began to wonder whether Capricaan would actually lead them into such bleak conditions, unprepared as they were. When they stopped to rest with the sun high above them, the boy turned to them and said:

"The entrance is just a little way ahead. Maybe another hour."

Jessie hesitated as she asked him:

"It wouldn't be a tunnel radiating a kind of blue light would it - leading into some sort of cavern?"

Capricaan said that it was, and wanted to know how she could possibly know that.

"I dreamt of being there," she said slowly to

them both. She closed her eyes as she recalled the nightmare in graphic detail, of the man dressed in black, pulling her fists apart as she described the head leaving the torso.

"It's just the stories from the village," Capricaan said to her, when she had finished. "They've got into your head."

"No, it's not," she told him, shaking away his words. "I'm sure it happened, or will happen."

"I've known these creatures for a long time. They're old; they're not capable of attacking anyone like that anymore. Once maybe..."

Jessie watched as the boy left his seat in frustration and started up the mountainside again. She glanced over at Luke. He seemed to be sharing the same thought - what if the cloned orkha that had brought them from Earth had found its way home to the Jume? They chose not to discuss it as they climbed. Capricaan kept his silence but stayed ahead of them, eager to disprove their fears. Only once did he turn round, when he reached the entrance to the cave, maybe a hundred yards below the first of the snow covering. His face bore a triumphant smirk, and as they clambered up over the last of the rocks to reach him, he stole out of the sun's warm light and into the cool blue incandescence of the cave.

Capricaan had already covered a lot of ground by the time Jessie and Luke took their first steps into the cave. She called out for him to wait for them but he either didn't hear or chose to ignore her. The sides of the tunnel were smooth and cold, the rock glimmering with an almost crystalline glitter that created its own light away from the sun's reach outside.

The air inside was crisp and fresh, and carried a sweet-smelling tang on a wind that circled around them, brushing their faces like a winter's caress.

The boy disappeared from sight as he turned a corner ahead of them, the patter of his feet echoing back off the walls. Jessie reached down and took hold of Luke's hand, his skin as cold as the rock around them, his fingers trembling. He looked at her, her smile calming the tense expression on his face.

"What is it?" she asked him.

His brow knitted again as he looked ahead.

"I'm not sure," he murmured. "But... it feels like I've been here before."

"You dreamt this place too?"

"No," he said. "Not dreamt. It's just... familiar somehow. I feel like I should know this place."

"You can't possibly have seen all this."

"I know, Jess," he conceded. "At least not with my eyes."

A scream from around the corner stole their attention and they took to their heels yelling the boy's name. By the time they reached him - slumped against the side of the tunnel, his hands bloody and clamped to his stomach - his scream had been reduced to laboured breaths. As he opened his mouth to speak, a trail of blood sputtered down over his chin and onto his chest. His eyes, wide and white, gazed up at them both.

"It rushed past me," he stammered, bubbles of blood gurgling between words on his lips. "So fast... I turned to open my arms..."

He took his hands from his stomach to show them. His belly had been sliced in several places, his innards slipping between them as he shuddered in pain.

"I saw black eyes..," he said quietly. "Black eyes and..." He clamped his hands over his stomach again, his fingers disappearing between the deepest of the lacerations. "It wasn't one of the older ones... was so fast..."

Jessie knelt beside him just as he coughed, a convulsion that shot another mouthful of blood out over himself. His eyes fluttered closed, the tremors in his body slowing until they finally ceased altogether. Jessie hung her head and felt Luke's hand on her shoulder. Pushing herself to her feet, she left Capricaan and continued deeper into the mountain.

"Where are you going?" Luke called out after her.

"Where do you think I'm going?"

"You can't be serious..."

"There's an orkha in there. Probably the same one that brought us here -"

"But you've seen what it can do..."

"The only hope we have for our future lies in facing that orkha, Luke. We must carry on."

Jessie slowed her pace as the tunnel began to grow wider, the cavern now visible just a little way ahead. Her feet resisted her as she caught sight of a heap of black rags only yards in front of her. As she approached the discarded sacking, she saw inside the battered and bloodied limbs and torso of the hunter. Her eyes followed the trail of scarlet across the floor to the head, her hand rising to stifle a sob as she caught its stare piercing blankly back at her.

She could feel Luke beside her now and took herself defiantly past the hunter and on into the cavern. Its high roof was vaulted and glittered with the same blue brilliance as the tunnel, illuminating the circular chamber and its countless catacombs and annexes, multi-layered and tiered around its walls. The knock of their footsteps echoed high up into the dome above them as they stepped cautiously around its perimeter staring into the catacombs, each one as empty as the next. They came upon a stairwell hewn into the rock leading down deeper into the mountain, and as they peered into its dark reaches, jumped as a strangled yell erupted from behind them. They had barely turned before they witnessed the beheading of the second black-robe, his skull hitting the floor inches from their feet and scuttling to the wall as its owner dropped like a sack of rotten fruit. Luke stumbled back, hitting the wall hard behind him, reeling as he lost his balance and tumbled down into the steep stairwell. Jessie reached after him, her eyes torn between the decapitated rider and his executioner, whose form had been a blur as it stole into one of the many vaults.

Her chest pounding, she hesitated at the top of the stairwell, unable to drag her eyes away from the point where the beast had disappeared. But before she could make a move in either direction, she was grabbed from behind and hauled back into a small oval vault.

She turned to lash out as her arms came free, her fists just missing the face of the third of the black-robed riders, the face of the leader she had not seen in her sleeping visions. But it was a face she knew only too well, despite being all but running with blood.

"What are you doing here?" Jessie demanded to know.

"I came back to finish what I started all those years ago," Kelso told her, grinning, his teeth also reddened with blood. "And there's just one more remaining."

"What about the old ones?"

"All dead."

Kelso pulled his gun from beneath his robes as he started back out into the cavern.

"You're crazy," Jessie said to him, following him out of the vault.

"Craziness is a disorder of intellect," Kelso corrected her. "My purpose is clear."

Jessie stayed at the edge of the cavern and watched as Kelso stepped out towards the centre, his gun poised in front of him, and yelled out to the creature of light. Almost immediately the still of the chamber began to stir, the air agitated by a wind beginning to circle, its pace quickening ever faster until he was standing alone inside the calm of a huge vortex, a single scream whining inside its storm.

Jessie took a step towards him as she saw him stumble as the vortex harried him, bustling him as it tried to take his legs from beneath him. Images began to appear inside the raging winds, snatches like flip-books of tiny black eyes, bloodied claws and needle teeth, ready to savour and to taste. The roar was deafening now, Kelso clamping his free hand to his head either to keep his sanity in or the rage of the orkha out.

"Where are you?" she heard him yell into the storm.

The storm answered him instantly, a blow from nowhere striking his chest hard and punching him to the ground. He scrambled to his knees, waving his gun in the air around him.

"Where are you?" he yelled again, firing into the tornado circling the cavern, once, twice, three times.

Again the storm answered, piercing his body from behind in a shower of scarlet rain before hauling him high into the vaulted roof above. His gun slipped from his fingers as he became part of the raging vortex, his body tumbling inside its grasp, his limbs as lifeless as a child's toy, as it carried him in its wild circles like detritus. Jessie could just hear his screams above the whining roar of the storm itself, and put her hands to her face as it suddenly released him. Kelso hit the wall of the chamber hard, coming apart instantly on impact in a smear of blood and scuffed cartilage. The storm died a heart beat later, and as Jessie turned, saw Luke standing at the top of the stairwell.

She went to call out to him but he was looking straight past her. She glanced behind her following his gaze, and there in the centre of the cavern stood the last of the orkhas. Nowhere to be seen was the vortex of screams, the rage of illusion. It simply stood, a glimmering blur of sinew, its torso striped like the children of Amst only far more frightening for its brutality. Its black eyes stared back unfeeling across the cavern, and as she followed them back to Luke, found that he had moved closer to enter such an arena.

Jessie now noticed that he had removed both his jacket and his shirt and was standing bare-chested. She almost choked as she saw how it too was marked; not stained with the grease paint of children's games but with the birthmark of a hybrid. She watched helplessly as he slowly walked towards the centre of the chamber, his face becoming clearer, tortured and wet with tears.

He paused as she called out to him.

"I now know who I am," he said to her.

"No," she said, shaking her head with despair. "You don't have to -"

"It won't let us leave, Jess, you know that as well as I. My whole life I've had questions with no one to answer them. Now I find the truth for myself."

Luke continued forward, ignoring Jessie's pleas as she called after him. Less than six feet from his adversary, he stopped, and there they stayed baring all against each other.

Jessie watched helplessly as the orkha began to secrete a watery fluid from its skin, a fluid that smouldered, curling around itself like a cloud of cobalt smoke. Horrified, she watched as Luke too began to envelop himself in the same smoke, fluid coming from his own flesh, the bodies and limbs of both becoming lost or merely hinted at inside the coiling vapour.

Soon the centre of the arena was but one ball of blue cloud, spiralling high up into the vaulted ceiling and trailing its fingers out to the very edges, its tang bitter on Jessie's tongue, sickening her belly. Keeping her eyes on the snatches of motion from within, she stumbled back and slumped against the cold rock. The movement inside the smoke started to quicken, sparks of light flashing now, charging the dense mist like an electrical storm. The cloud began to move to a single rhythm now, turning, twisting, winding, steadily faster like a cyclone, the lightning flashing in the lines of the smoke with ever increasing intensity, burning white with almost primeval energy.

Such was the power caged inside this tornado, that Jessie covered her head with her arms when the first of the guttural screams came, deafening angry screams that pierced the air of the cavern, rebounding off the walls like bullets. Livid rages came also as the battle of claw and flesh erupted, the lightning unleashing lethal fingers of burning energy out of the sparking indigo cloud, striking the cavern walls and sending shards of rock crashing to the ground.

Yet more lightning came, cracking the ceiling overhead, columns of blue toppling like vast city buildings. Jessie cried out as one of the walls above her came apart, shattering as it landed just yards from her feet. She looked around her and saw one of the vaults was only a short distance from her. Rocks were crashing all around her now, but she had to reach it.

The barks and screams were whistling

headlong in the fiery air now, battering and pounding her with their incessant assault. Ducking into the opening of the vault, she yelled out as something hit the wall above her, falling onto her head before hitting the ground.

She swiped it away as she stumbled to the floor, her hand coming away hot and wet. Looking down she saw it was the arm of the orkha, glistening blue and scarlet, its fist still clenching a wad of black hair.

She pushed it away with revulsion, only noticing then from the chill of the wind that her face was also wet. Putting her fingers to it, she brought them away red and gummy, but the flow from the severed limb was still running its course and found her lips before she could wipe it away, its sickly aroma already on her tongue.

Peering out into the arena she could see the cavern floor awash with pools of blood between the swirling tendrils of smoke. The harried screams were rocking in pitch now, one heightening into further frenzy as the other became choked and strangled as though drowning in a mire. The lightning was coming in blinding sheets, filling the chamber, making it painful for Jessie to see, but she held on long enough for the final blow.

A raging bellow filled the air with its

thunder, the second strangled cry disappearing beneath a deluge of viscous fluid. The lightning paled then ceased, the tornado calmed, and the blue smoke curled up upon itself, until everything was silent except for the patter of the last few remaining rocks tumbling to the ground.

Jessie tried to haul herself up, straining to see into the reaches of the maelstrom, now itself fading and disappearing. Dark shapes were becoming visible now, twisted limbs bent and awkward, yet only one chest lay heaving. From where she was inside the vault she could make out very little, both figures saturated in blood, both flanked with stripes of their breed. But very slowly one started to move, pushing itself with great effort to its feet. Stumbling it turned to face her, a rain of scarlet dropping from the motion. Still she could not distinguish the figure, its flesh still radiating like blurred light. It made little difference, however, for it had seen her and was now stepping towards her.

Jessie pushed herself back into the vault, not daring to breathe, nor even to think if it were the orkha, the last of its species. It was the last thing standing between life and extinction, and surely with such responsibility and fear would come anger and brutality.

Her back pressed hard against the cold rock, her eyes clenched against the inevitable, she waited helplessly. Paralysed and without a weapon, she shuddered as she heard the slap of its feet on the wet floor approaching from the cavern, an inconsistent pattern as it shuffled wounded or indeed close to death itself. Whichever it might have been became no hope for salvation as the footsteps suddenly came to a staggered halt beside her, accompanied by a tiny dripping sound like raindrops pattering on soft earth.

She sobbed as she looked up, awaiting the certain blow that would take her head from her shoulders. But it did not come. Through the stream of her tears she could make out the battered face of Luke, ravaged beneath a mask of blackening blood, devoid of expression but for his eyes that soothed her fear. He went to bend down to her, but his legs buckled beneath him and he collapsed in front of her. She could see his body had been opened up in a number of places, blackened and raw, but he seemed either too numb or tired to care or simply had the will of the last of his breed burning inside him.

He looked up at her as he put his hand to her face, his fingers leaving tracks of red on her cheek, but it was bliss just to feel his touch on her skin once again.

"It's over," he said to her softly.

"What happens now?"

"I don't know," he replied, shaking his head, which only dizzied his thoughts further. "I didn't even know I was capable of what just happened."

"And yet you went to face it."

"What choice did I have, Jess? This place has energy, and I could feel it - still can feel it - charging me, burning through me. I feel as though I should know more than I do, but..."

"So what about us?" she said suddenly.

Luke glanced at her quizzically.

"You stay here and I go back, is that it?

"In the lightning I saw glimpses of history, the past and the future. I saw other worlds," he was grinning now, a wide scarlet smile, but the pain wracked in his body was still hindering his excitement. "Don't you see, Jess, there are secrets to be found here, lessons to be learnt -"

"For you, maybe -"

"For us." Luke took her hands in his, wincing in pain as he did so. "Come with me, Jess. There is so much to see, so much to experience. I want us to see it all together."

"I don't think you're in any condition to go

anywhere," she said to him. "You'll have to heal yourself first."

"The process has already begun," he replied, his grin on his face once again.

His confidence in everything he was ignorant of seemed foolish and yet she could not stop herself breaking a smile also. The blue rock of the Jume brought only the light for her to see by; was it indeed possible that it could bring to Luke the light of discovery and promise? She had crossed a bridge into a world she didn't know existed; could it therefore be possible to uncover or build new bridges to yet more worlds?

Jessie wondered as she helped Luke struggle to his feet, if such promise was restricted for only those touched by the energy of the orkha, or whether it had always been there just waiting for anyone to find.

She smiled as she watched him close his eyes, feeling the strength of the Jume run through him, and was glad that they had neither a microscope nor a tape measure between them. From now on they would have faith in the essence of life, and live it as though each day was their last, and each breath bought a new beginning.

The End

Ascension

Paul Stuart Kemp

Hampton, England 1172: After witnessing the death of her family in a frenzied witch-drowning ritual, Gaia, an eight year old girl, flees for her life. Alone and afraid, she stumbles upon a magical young boy who takes her on a journey to meet Calista, a spirit capable of harnessing both dreams and time, with promises of so much more.

Makara, Kenya 2589: There are desperate times at the end of the human race. Kiala is a man living at one of the last stations on Earth, a planet where all life has been eradicated by snow and ice. With his future hinted at, could he hold the key to preserving what little life remains, and if so, why is Calista intent on stopping him?

London, England 1994: When Carly Maddison's fiance is suddenly abducted under very strange circumstances and her fleeing brother is accused of his demise, she finds herself trapped in the depths of a dark and secret world. Her love for them both draws her deeper into that world, and if she is to discover both its rules and, ultimately, its solution, then she must face the past as well as the future, in order to learn truths that she would previously have thought unimaginable.

Witchcraft, alien abduction, ritual murders; all unfathomable mysteries, all with a human heart. Paul Stuart Kemp's science fiction horror fantasy takes the reader on an extraordinary journey, where such mysteries are found to be sown into the human soul, unable to be removed, and unable to be revoked.

ISBN 0 9538215 0 1

Bloodgod

Paul Stuart Kemp

An archaeological expedition to a desert region uncovers both an ancient temple with strange hieroglyphics as well as an old man with a story to tell. Merriach speaks of a creature that decimated most of two tribes, and relays the whereabouts of a magical box that contains the Master of Kar'mi'shah. He has remained in isolation inside the buried temple for hundreds of years, waiting for the tribes to return, and for someone to release his Master.

Jenner Hoard is a thief recently released from prison. Montague, his benefactor, does not want him to quit working for him, and already has two lucrative jobs lined up for an anonymous customer, a deal involving the Blood Of The Ancients, and the theft of a mysterious box from an apartment building in London.

Times have never been more desperate for the vampire community living in the darkest depths of London. Alexia is one such vampire who has a brutal encounter with The Howler of Westminster after a butchered corpse is found floating in the Thames.

Human vampire hunters, known as Skulkers, have become more skillful and connected over the years, and find easy prey in those demons who are too careless about their actions. Join Alexia as she struggles to survive in a dark and foreboding world, where even demons suffer anguish, and in death there is still a fight.

ISBN 0 9538215 2 8

The Unholy

Paul Stuart Kemp

In an old forester's cottage in rural southern England, Irene and Michael Rider, a young married couple, decide one night to 'play the ouija'. What they invite into their new home begins to take its toll not only on their lives, but also on the lives of those around them, and the lives of their, as yet, unborn children.

Trapped in a world in which they no longer have choices, they struggle to raise the idyllic family of which they've always dreamed.

The birds in the trees are watching them, waiting for some eternal event, but the ancient evil that sits behind their eyes has time on its hands, time enough to wait forever.

Paul Stuart Kemp is one of England's darkest writers. The Unholy takes the reader into his darkest world yet; a place of demonic possession, of nightmarish visions and creatures, and the destruction of an entire family. But only at the heart of this world can true values be found: the resilience of love, the sanctity of marriage, and what it means to be human.

ISBN 0 9538215 4 4